DISCOVERED SECRETS

DISCOVERED SECRETS

THE DISCOVERED TRUTH SERIES ROMANTIC SUSPENSE
BOOK ONE

JULIE BAWDEN DAVIS

DISCOVERED SECRETS

ISBN-13: 978-1-7337505-7-8

ISBN-10: 1-7337505-7-6

Distributed by Roses Are Red Publishing

rosesareredpublishing.com

❀ Created with Vellum

ACKNOWLEDGMENTS

As they say, it takes a village. Here's my village. I'm supremely grateful to each of these fabulous people!

ARC Reading Gems

Julie Schlueter

Beth Helm

Tara Bradley

Angela Barnes

Heather Wamboldt

Kery Bailey

Trish Darrenkamp

Marilyn Smith

Lisa Starkey

Susa Fraccaroli

Amber Mancebo

Ellen White

Pros

Sharon Whatley, editing

Judy Bullard, cover design

Kayla Curry, logo design

Kyle Kane, logo design

Sabrina Wildermuth, design consultation

Jeremy Davis, book design

To Zonians everywhere, and to my "Navy brat" sisters, Amy, Mandy, and Katie.

AUTHOR'S NOTE

Some Zonians say that when you drink from the Chagres River, like a first love, the experience forever infuses within you the desire to return to a unique place in time. I know this happened to me when I lived in the Panama Canal Zone, a forty-by-ten-mile strip of tropical paradise that ran through the country of Panama and was supplied by the Chagres. There, for a brief period in the late 1970s and early 1980s, I embraced a near Utopian way of life that as a "Navy brat" I haven't to this day experienced anywhere else.

Today, the Canal Zone is but a memory. On September 7, 1977, President Jimmy Carter signed the Torrijos-Carter Treaties that forever altered the future of the 75,000 American expats who had lived in this United States territory over a span of seventy-four years. The treaties dissolved the Canal Zone and transferred operation of the Panama Canal from the US to Panama. Many former Zonians emigrated to the United States, like the main character in this book.

I lived in the Canal Zone from 1979-1981 when I was in my late teens —just prior to the treaty taking effect and shortly thereafter. The events in this book are based on fact, but the characters and stories, while entirely fictional, are a result of that time and place and the unique experiences I encountered with the special spirit and people of the Canal Zone and Panama.

PROLOGUE

The rain pelted the *bohío's* thatched roof, and Jesse McMillan sighed as the humidity seeped into his pores. For a microsecond, the midday tropical storm stilled the aching in his gut, but the wrenching on his insides returned as he watched through the liquid curtain the tropical land he loved and would soon lose. How he wanted to stand here forever. At least until someone told him Carter wouldn't sign the treaty that would take away his home.

Hearing a cough, Jesse turned to find Randy Strickland shaking himself off and wiping wisps of red hair out of his face.

"Earth to Jesse! I walked right by you. Where the hell were you?" Randy asked.

Jesse shrugged. "Nowhere."

"Sometimes I worry."

"You, worry? Yeah, right," Jesse said and snorted.

"What's that supposed to mean?" Randy pulled a rumpled Marlboro pack out of his jeans pocket and extracted a joint. "I'm a serious individual."

Jesse ignored Randy's lame stab at humor. "Any word from Sam?"

"No. He's probably hiding out with some buddies and won't come out until the heat's off."

Jesse leaned on the edge of the picnic table that sat under the *bohío*, gazing out at the gauzy, green landscape. "It's been three weeks, Randy. He's probably hidden deep in a Panamanian jail, or maybe he's tied to cement blocks in the canal."

"Don't talk that way, man. You can be a real downer." Randy took two deep tokes of the joint and offered it to Jesse.

"No, thanks." Jesse fanned the sweet smell of marijuana out of his face.

Randy raised his eyebrows. "Look, you worry too much. Everything's under control. Sam will be back soon. I know it."

"You don't worry enough," said Jesse. "You're playing it way too close."

Randy's thin face puckered as he took another toke. Half-moons rimmed the underside of his eyes from late nights partying.

"Listen, as soon as Sam gets back, our operation will be back to normal."

"Nothing is ever going to be back to normal," said Jesse.

"You mean the treaty? Things won't change that much. It'll be business as usual. Once a Zonian, always a Zonian. Right?"

Jesse opened his mouth to answer, but shut it. Randy obviously didn't feel the same fist in his heart. He wasn't on the same brakeless, downhill ride Jesse had been on ever since they heard about the treaty signing.

"Your problem is that you're just too stressed out, Jess. Stay mellow. Things will be cool. You'll see," Randy intoned as he blew a fat, clumsy smoke ring into the heavy air.

The sky rumbled, making conversation impossible. Just as well. Jesse watched transfixed as rain thrashed the leaves of a nearby palm tree, announcing that things would never be the same.

1

IRVINE, CALIFORNIA, DECEMBER 20, 1989

Jesse stood at the stove waiting for his grilled cheese to toast to golden perfection. With a spatula, he edged up a corner and peeked below. Not yet. Plucking a dart out of the board on his kitchen wall, he stepped back, aimed at Jimmy Carter's forehead, and let it fly.

"Bull's-eye," he yelled, hitting the former president's photo in between the eyes. Millicent, Jesse's cat, didn't flinch. She continued nibbling the food he'd just dropped onto her plate in the corner of the small condo kitchen.

Jesse periodically changed Carter's photo, because the former peanut farmer would become unrecognizable. Friends from Panama always threw a dart at him, often before they even got a beer. They'd curse him for signing the treaties that gave their home, the Canal Zone, an idyllic Mayberry-like, tropical community, back to the Panamanians.

He inspected the grilled cheese again. Perfect. Turning off the stove, he slid the sandwich out of the pan and onto a paper towel. Waiting only a couple of seconds for it to cool, he took a big bite, immediately regretting his impatience when the hot, melted cheese coated his tongue. He started to reach into the cupboard for a glass to get some water, but the phone rang, so he grabbed the receiver instead.

"McMillan here."

"Where the hell are you? You should be in here pounding out a page-turner on Panama, and why the hell isn't that 'kids on crack cocaine' story on my desk?"

Jesse turned on the tap and leaned over the sink to cup a handful of water in an attempt to cool the burn left on his tongue. "I'm working on it." He tried to sound convincing. The clock on the stove said nine. His boss, Burt Williams, was working late. "What's up?"

"You're kidding, right? What planet you on? Panama's upside down. I need copy now. Pull your head out of your ass and tell me you can come up with something besides an, 'I'm scratching my balls news flash.' You lived in Panama, McMillan. I want inside dirt. Pronto."

"I lived in the Canal Zone," corrected Jesse, his chest tightening at the mention of his childhood home.

"Yeah, in a colony right down the center of Panama, so don't tell me you never took a walk on the wild side."

Burt was obviously fired up.

"What's going on there?"

"An off-duty Marine was shot and that dictator Noriega annulled the recent election, so the US sent in thousands of our soldiers to get things under control in Panama and arrest him for drug trafficking, but he's on the loose. Panama is getting hit hard. The troops even bombed parts of el Chorrillo. Now the area is burning, and locals are looting. President Bush is calling it Operation Just Cause."

Jesse didn't respond.

"You still there? Turn on the damn TV and tune into the rest of the world." His boss sounded exasperated. "Then shake it off and get your carcass in here."

Jesse hung up and flipped on his television set. Sure enough, Panama filled just about every channel, replacing the Christmas programming that would have been on. A knot formed in his stomach as he strained to spot landmarks amidst the rioters swarming the streets while smoke billowed from burning buildings—a crappy way to see his former home after nearly a decade away from it.

. . .

When Jesse arrived in the *LA Times* newsroom a half hour later and headed for his desk, Phil, the city news reporter, announced, "You finally decided to wake up and show up. Burt's been threatening to send a warrant out for you. I'm stuck here waiting on word from a source about a burglary in Santa Ana's city hall. If I were you, I would have been here hours ago. At this rate, you're going to miss the scoop altogether."

Only about thirty-five, Phil had a tendency to hunch forward. That and thinning blond hair made him look like someone teetering on the edge of fifty. Since Jesse arrived at the paper five years before, Phil begrudged him. He had wanted the investigative Latin-American beat that Jesse landed because of his ability to speak Spanish and connection to Panama. Full of action and drama, like drug busts and mafia-style murders, some days Jesse would love to give the beat to Phil—especially his recent story.

At first, Jesse felt excited about the idea of uncovering the drug epidemic among kids on the streets of Santa Ana. Since studying journalism in college and learning about the profession's idols—investigative reporters who won Pulitzer Prizes for stories about social injustices, like foster care system abuse and the plight of immigrant sweatshop workers—he'd dreamed of fearlessly digging for the truth and exposing reality on paper. He also wanted to do some good, and he figured if he could shine a light on kids as young as eleven hooked on heavy drugs, then maybe he could make a difference.

Crossing fine lines turned out to be more exciting and fulfilling in his daydreams, though. Jesse thought about the sideways eye he found himself turning to rampant illegal drugs while working this story. The kids he'd seen hopped up on crack cocaine, a highly addictive street drug that had ravaged the barrio in recent years, haunted him and made him want to try to help every last one of them. He told a friend who worked at Social Services about the plight of the strung out kids when he interviewed him for his expert opinion, but some days Jesse wondered what the hell he was doing. All this for a good story? Was it even frigging worth it to wrestle with his conscience on a daily basis? To top off this shit show, as he interviewed drug users and low-level dealers, the name Gonzales kept coming up. The grapevine identified him as a Mexican mafia drug lord, but whether he supplied the steady stream of crack was unclear.

One day, as Jesse sat in the newsroom transcribing interview tapes, someone identifying himself as the right-hand man of Gonzales called Jesse with a message. Jorge Hernandez told Jesse that Gonzales wanted to set the record straight. He insisted that he had nothing to do with the sale of drugs to minors and wanted to go on the record stating just that. Initially, Jesse's blood raced when he thought about quoting Gonzales in his story. Even Burt became excited at the idea—a feat for someone who only seemed to know cranky as his default. So far, even though Gonzales supposedly wanted to talk, Jesse had only gotten quotes from Jorge, who kept insisting that *el Jefe* was too busy right now. Burt would freak if he knew that Jesse didn't have any direct quotes from Gonzales yet. He jumped in his seat when his boss's paunch appeared next to his head.

"Tell me the crack cocaine story is just about wrapped up and you can put everything you've got into writing the inside scoop on Panama. I want a page-one view from the trenches that's going to sell papers. One of the reasons I put you on this beat was because of your connection to Panama—so use it."

"I don't know, boss. It's been awhile since I lived there."

"You shitting me, McMillan? You're a Zonian, for crying out loud. Get on the horn and get me something that will make me look good with the publisher."

"Have I ever let you down?" asked Jesse, injecting more conviction into his tone than he felt.

"No, and don't start. I want something on Panama before the 3:00 am cutoff. And I want a draft of the drug story on my desk by nine in the morning—with some juicy quotes from Gonzales. You've been working on it for weeks. I don't care if you're still hammering away when the sun comes up." Burt lumbered back into his office and slammed the door.

Other reporters liked to hope that Burt was simply bluster. They found it difficult to believe he could be as callous as he sounded, but Jesse discovered his boss to be pretty transparent. Over the last five years, Jesse and Burt had worked many late nights together, because the investigative work didn't sleep. A couple of years ago, Jesse had a bird's-eye view of Burt's marriage falling apart. When the newsroom quieted down and it was just him and his boss, Jesse couldn't help but overhear the late night calls. At first his boss apologized for not being home, but over time the exchanges turned nasty, and Jesse eventually heard Burt snarling about what sounded like suspicions of another man. Despite his personal troubles, or maybe because of them, Burt was Jesse's best editor ever. When he finished with Jesse's copy, it couldn't sound any better. Burt was smart, though, and it was just a matter of time before he found out the truth—that Jesse hadn't even gotten close to Gonzales yet.

Picking up the phone, Jesse dialed his parents' number.

"Mom."

"You're calling late. Everything okay?"

"Yeah, fine. How's dad?"

"His back is bothering him again."

"What do the doctors say?"

"That he needs to get off his behind and do some exercise."

"I'm sure you heard about Panama," Jesse interjected.

"Of course, it's all over the news. Your dad insisted on skipping our walk to watch it on TV. What a terrible Christmas present for Panama."

"The paper wants me to write a piece—the inside story and all that. Who do we know who still lives there?"

He could picture his mom sitting down at the kitchen table and putting her reading glasses on with one hand, as if they would help her think better.

"Well, you know Lorraine Peterson and her folks—" his mom started, but he cut her off.

"I don't want to call them, Mom. Anyone else?"

"I've never understood that. You and Lorraine used to be such good friends. You grew up together, for Heaven's sake. What on earth happened?"

"It's a long story, and I've got a lot of work to do."

Jesse's mom sighed. "You always say that. The Madisons moved to the States several years ago. The Edgewoods left Panama a couple of years ago, too. I know! The Myers. They're still there!"

Of course, Micky Myers lived near Jesse here in California, and they went out partying together sometimes. He told Jesse that his parents refused to leave what was left of the Zone.

After getting the Myers' number and promising to visit his parents soon, Jesse looked at the clock—eleven. Two in the morning in Panama. He'd have to wait three or four hours. As he remembered, Mr. Myers was an early bird. In the meantime, Jesse would check wire copy and get some background information. He could talk to Micky's father as soon as possible and plug his quotes in quickly.

Before he got started, Jesse made a quick run to the cafeteria. Only one thing could get him through the night—a heart-jolting cup of black coffee.

By two-thirty in the morning, Jesse had pieced together an impressive background story on the Canal Zone, Panama and Noriega. Thanks to a tip from a *New York Times* correspondent in Panama, Jesse contacted a Latin America political analyst who was up at 5 am East Coast time. After that call, he dialed the Myers' number. Mr. Myers answered on the second ring.

"This is Jesse McMillan. I'm a friend of your son, Micky. My parents—"

"Tim and Susie McMillan's son, of course. What's going on? Everything okay there in California? Micky okay?"

"Yes, sir, sorry to bother you this early, and no worries about Micky. He's doing great. And my parents are fine. They're still in Sherman Oaks, where we moved in '82 when we left the Zone."

"Well, super. How can I help you? I guess you've heard about the Zone and Panama? But then none of us are surprised about the rioting. There's been unrest bubbling here ever since they let Noriega take over."

"That's why I'm calling, sir. I'm a reporter with the *LA Times* now, and I've been assigned to write a story about what's going on there. I was hoping you could help by answering some questions."

"Why sure, son. If we get cut off, don't think I hung up on you. The lines have been unreliable since the riots started yesterday."

Micky's dad proceeded to tell Jesse about how even before the riots, the Zone had begun a descent from its former glory. He spoke of how the once pristine, secluded enclave, where the residents known as Zonians and military families had lived carefree, sheltered lives, slowly gave way to a community of American expatriates living a precarious existence amidst an unsettled third-world country.

"The irony is that we used to worry about the Panamanians screwing up Canal operations and causing ships to collide and sink," he said. "Now we're sitting in the middle of a war zone. The troops have the Zone locked down and are keeping it relatively safe, but there's always collateral damage. And the streets of Panama are heartbreaking. It's going to take the downtown area years to recover. They literally bombed parts of el Chorrillo trying to root out Noriega, and a lot of the area has burned down. I've only ventured out of the Zone briefly, and what I saw I could barely believe. Cars burned and turned on their sides. Storefront windows shattered and shops ransacked. I saw a kid no more than fifteen years old smash a clothing store window with a tire iron that he probably stole from the car he destroyed. Those poor merchants."

Jesse's heart raced as Micky's dad went on to tell him about the gunshots close to his house yesterday and how he found a bullet embedded in the stucco. Even though Jesse worried about his former home and old friends who still lived there, Mr. Myers' words thrilled him, because the quotes promised to make great copy. Burt would be pleased. Perhaps pleased enough to give Jesse a little more time on the Gonzales story. He could dream.

By three o'clock in the morning, with exhausted elation, Jesse put the finishing touches on the article, printed it out and brought it into Burt's office. "You slid in here on one cheek," Burt growled as he snatched the manuscript from him. Jesse waited, holding his breath as Burt reviewed the article and breathed a deep sigh of relief when his boss called typesetting with approval. At 4:15 am, the story would be out the door in the morning paper.

"Good job, McMillan," Burt said as he headed for the elevator and no doubt home. "Dynamo quotes from the guy still in Panama."

The elevator opened and Burt stepped in, pushing the button. "Now get to work on the Gonzales story. I'll be expecting it when I get in," he barked.

Jesse sighed. No point thinking about sleep tonight. Burt meant it about the story. He'd demoted and even fired reporters for not meeting deadlines. Jesse refused to give Phil the satisfaction of taking over the Latin America beat while he slunk to something soft like urban affairs.

He planned to spice up the Gonzales draft he'd already written—adding some teasers to interest Burt. Then his boss would ask for additions, which would buy Jesse time to figure out how in the hell he could get to Gonzales.

Better not go home—the bed would tempt him, and he'd never make his deadline if he slept for a couple of hours. Much worse to get up exhausted from a deep sleep to work, anyway. Doing that made him feel more sleep-deprived than if he simply stayed awake. A night owl, Jesse could easily stay up on a regular basis to two or three in the morning, but this would be an all-nighter.

By seven, Jesse had finished. The story had zip, and he'd patched weaker areas with some good doubletalk that he hoped would make Burt scratch his head while Jesse got to Gonzales.

After he printed out the story and put it in Burt's office, Jesse sat down at his desk to brainstorm about accessing Gonzales, but Becky, one of the paper's political reporters, soon interrupted him.

"Jesse, have you been here all night? Did you make your deadline?"

He nodded and yawned.

An early bird, Becky perched on the edge of Jesse's desk and pecked the floor with her foot, which annoyed him, but did serve to wake him up further.

She always dressed conservatively in tailored dresses and practical black pumps and wore her brown hair in a tight bun. Once when he asked her about her "uniform," she became defensive and told him that she wanted to blend in with the political types, but he guessed that her appearance made her feel in control. A few times Jesse got the hint that she might be interested in him, but she was totally not his type and smart enough to pick up on that.

"You better go home and get some sleep," she said, springing up from his desk and hurrying to her own. "I've got to call a senator before he heads into meetings for the day."

Even if he was interested in Becky, Raquel had taught him to avoid mixing business with pleasure. She had worked at a rival newspaper. Things started hot and intense with Raquel, but before long plummeted to macabre. Her disturbing behavior included calling him incessantly after their first date and even waiting for him at his front door when he went out with Micky. She said she came to apologize, but Jesse knew she wanted to see if he brought a woman home with him.

That was only the beginning of weird. She refused to let up—swinging from crazed, unfounded jealousy to remorseful oceans of tears. Finally, one night Jesse no longer cared how great the sex was. His worst enemy could have her. He just wanted her out of his life for good. That evening in her apartment, Jesse broke up with her, only to find her sobbing outside his door an hour later. He still got silent calls in the middle of the night.

The truth was that experience disappointed Jesse. Not because he broke it off with Raquel. She definitely was a certified wack job. He was just so tired of being alone. It's not something he'd admit to his guy friends, and it even felt corny acknowledging it to himself, but Jesse really wanted a girl who felt like home. Someone steady, caring and sexy all rolled into one, who understands herself and feels comfortable in her own skin. He'd only known one girl like that, and it had been almost ten years since he'd seen her. She could be on the other side of the world, for all he knew.

Becky hung up from her phone call and began chattering about the senator having had a heart attack. Jesse smiled at her, half listening, and then felt his blood pressure rise at the sight of the flashing cursor on his computer screen. He'd soon have his own heart attack if he didn't figure out how to talk to Gonzales pronto. The only way in was through Jorge. That meant smacking himself awake and picking up the phone for what could end up being a frustrating and futile call.

2

Jesse took a sip of bitter, cold coffee, grimacing as the acrid liquid snaked its way down his throat, then dialed a Santa Ana number.

"*Bueno?*" said the voice on the other end of the line.

"Jorge, *por favor.*"

"*Quien llama?*"

"Jesse McMillan."

"*Un momento.*"

A couple of minutes later, Jorge's voice, with its usual who-the-fuck's-bothering-me tone, filled the phone line. "*Qué pasa?*"

"We need to meet," said Jesse.

"What the hell for?"

"This is *importante,*" Jesse said. "When can we meet?"

"Things are shit out there right now. Go on vacation. Get laid, McMillan."

"I can't go anywhere until I finish this story. My boss is on my ass, threatening to pull the whole thing, if I don't answer some more questions. Just hear me out."

"*Mierda.* Okay, okay. Meet me at el Bistec on Grand at ten this morning," Jorge said. "They're closed until noon, but the owner will know you're coming."

"Thanks, man, I owe you."

"You got that right," said Jorge, leaving Jesse with a dial-tone in his ear.

He looked at the clock—only a couple of hours before he had to leave. More coffee would just do a number on his stomach. Instead, he decided to close his eyes for a few minutes. He must have fallen asleep, because he jumped in his seat when Burt smacked him on the top of his head with a wad of papers and threw them on Jesse's desk. His article, marked up in angry red pen.

"What the hell is this?" Burt asked. "Gonzales doesn't say shit in here."

"What did you expect him to say?" said Jesse. "I traffic drugs to children. Let me incriminate myself?"

Burt's eyes narrowed. "I know you, McMillian. There's something you're not telling me. Out with it."

Jesse's exhausted mind groped for a plausible answer.

"Did he threaten you? Is that it?"

"Something like that," Jesse lied.

"What the hell is that supposed to mean? I'm getting really pissed here, McMillan. I let you invest the last three weeks in this story, and now I'm hearing about you being threatened. It's turning out to be a bunch of bullshit. Wallerstein expects something big, and you give me this."

Mentioning the publisher meant his boss felt pressured. Not good. The other reporters pretended to work, but Jesse knew they had their antennas tuned in to his and Burt's conversation.

"Can we talk in private, boss?"

"This better be good."

The newsroom watched as they walked toward Burt's office.

"What the hell are you all gawking at?" Burt yelled. "Get to work, or tomorrow's headline will read, 'Reporters Thrown Out of Window, One by One.'"

After shutting his office door, Burt sat down behind his massive desk buried in stacks of books and manuscripts and topped off by a half dozen dirty coffee cups. Crossing his arms, he leaned back in his chair and said, "Level with me."

"Okay, Gonzales has sort of threatened me, but I can work it out. Give me some time."

"Sort of threatened you? Is that like sort of drunk or sort of dead?"

"Okay, he gave me some shit," Jesse continued with the lie. "He was fine with the story until just recently, and then he got weird about it. I've got to check it out more. Give me a couple more weeks, and I'll have a winner on your desk."

Burt grunted. "I always wondered how you were going to pull this off, McMillan. No one has ever even seen Gonzales and certainly hasn't gotten him on record. You told me it was going good, so that's why I promised Wallerstein something major." His boss sat silent for a few moments and then leaned forward, his hooded eyes boring into Jesse's bleary ones. "I better not regret this. And you damn well better not get yourself killed. You've got one week."

"You won't regret it, boss. Scout's honor."

"Scout's honor? Go home and get some sleep, McMillan."

Jesse left Burt's office and sat down at his desk, their final exchange lingering in his mind. He chuckled at having said, "Scout's honor," and then smiled when he recalled a mid-1970s afternoon in Panama.

"Haven't you figured out by now that Boy Scouts are totally uncool, Jess?" It was the beginning of tenth grade. He and Randy stood in front of Balboa High School in the Canal Zone while students poured out the doors. Most of the younger kids headed home on foot or by bike, while the seniors got into their cars. Randy lit a cigarette, inhaled and blew out a cloud of smoke. "Let's skip Scouts and go smoke joints at the Causeway."

"Forget it. I'm supposed to get my fishing badge today. I worked hard for that," said Jesse.

"You can get it next time."

Jesse thought about it for a second. "It won't be the same thing."

"Man, sometimes you're like an old woman."

"You don't care because you haven't earned even one badge," said Jesse.

"You know," Randy said, gesturing with the cigarette, "Who cares if you can tie a square knot? Rolling a joint is a hell of a lot more useful."

Jesse looked sideways at his friend and raised his eyebrows.

"Yeah, well, I'll go to Scouts if you agree on one thing," said Randy.

"What?"

"Don't call it Boy Scouts again, just Scouts, and for crying out loud, don't ever tell Sam and the guys that we didn't quit this year like I told them we were going to."

"Did you know that a lot of famous people were Eagle Scouts, like Neil Armstrong and President Ford?"

"I guess I wasn't listening at that meeting," said Randy as he flicked his cigarette into the street and took off down the palm-tree-lined sidewalk. "Step on a crack, break your mother's back!" he yelled, stomping on each fissure.

Jesse followed his friend, careful to avoid each crack.

At 10 am sharp, Jesse arrived outside the restaurant and looked around for Jorge's car. No sign of it. Approaching the deteriorating, charcoal-black building, he looked up above the door to see that the painted "el" in el Bistec had faded nearly beyond recognition. He knocked several times.

"Who is it?"

"Jesse McMillan."

The door opened and a short Mexican man in a one-size-too-big business suit let Jesse in and then slammed and locked the door behind him.

The sound of the lock engaging made Jesse catch his breath. This could easily be a setup. Jesse hadn't slept in more than twenty-four hours, and the stupidity that comes with fatigue could get him killed. He massaged a kink in the back of his neck.

"Relax at the bar, *Señor*. Can I offer you a drink?" the man said in stilted English. With his blond hair, blue eyes and six-foot, lanky build, Jesse didn't look like someone who spoke Spanish. Though he generally made his bilingual status known, in this instance he decided to keep that to himself. If involved in an ambush, it wasn't much, but at least he'd have that in his back pocket.

A soda or coffee would give Jesse a much needed pick-me-up and stimulate his brain, but he decided he better blend in, so he asked for a beer and sat down at the bar to wait for Jorge, Gonzales's right-hand man. The two had met a few weeks before after Jorge had phoned Jesse in the newsroom. Jesse had arrived early to the Costa Mesa diner where they'd agreed to meet and had second thoughts when the Mexican bull charged through the front door and descended on the booth where he sat waiting. Jesse swore his nostrils flared as he lowered his hulking frame into the bench across from him.

At that first meeting, Gonzales's protector and no-nonsense PR person proceeded to order a steak burrito and then grill Jesse about his background. As Jesse answered questions about moving up the ranks at a weekly paper and then transitioning to the *Times*, he thought about how Jorge had certainly checked him out prior to their meeting and already knew all of these things. He figured it must be his way of corroborating Jesse's story. As a reporter, he could understand that.

"Our business, if we had one, never sells to kids," said Jorge, "*Nunca!*" he repeated in Spanish for emphasis. "*El Jefe* has a wife and children of his own. Hell, so do I. And we have no patience where that's concerned. You make sure to print that."

Jesse took notes as Jorge talked, but avoided being bamboozled by the man's words.

"You say that children are off *el Jefe's* radar, but we both know that kids *are* doing drugs on the streets of Santa Ana. So how are they getting the drugs?" Jesse tried not to gulp as Jorge took a big bite of his burrito and washed it down with half a beer before answering.

"There are plenty of lowlife players on the street, who don't care where the money comes from. We know who they are."

"And?"

"And nothing. There's also plenty of the same scum throughout South America, where a lot of the stuff is coming from. Talk about pushing kids to do drugs. In many countries the kids are the drug mules."

A loud rapping on el Bistec's door pulled Jesse back to the present. The restaurant's owner scuttled aside after opening the door for Jorge, who strode across the room and yanked a bar stool toward him to sit down near Jesse. Grabbing the beer the owner had left on the bar moments before he arrived, Jorge squeezed a lime into the neck of the bottle and took a long pull of the frothy liquid. Then he slammed the half-drained bottle down and swung to face Jesse.

"*Amigo*, we meet again." Jorge's baritone voice filled the near empty room.

"Wife and kids okay?" Jesse asked, not wanting to jump right in.

"The kids, they drive me nuts, and the wife, she talks too damn much and spends *demasiado* money. Especially at this time of year." He laughed and took another gulp of the beer. "So what's so *importante*?"

Jesse took a quick breath and blurted, "I have to meet Gonzales."

Jorge spit beer into the air and wiped his mouth with the back of his hand.

"You *loco, gringo*? Nobody meets *el Jefe*!"

"If I can't meet him, how am I supposed to know he really exists?" asked Jesse, bracing himself for Jorge's response. "Maybe you made him up."

Jorge extended a giant black leather boot and stomped on a cockroach scurrying across the floor. "You think I make him up like I make up bedtime stories for my kids?"

"It's my boss. He won't print a word without direct quotes from *el Jefe*."

Jorge looked away. "Get the hell out of here and write your story, *amigo*."

"I can't. The newspaper is screwed if Gonzales comes forward and says I never talked to him," said Jesse. "This is standard procedure."

"*Mierda*, you're like my wife. I do so much for you, and all you want is more."

"I don't have a story right now," said Jesse. "I have paper I can wipe my ass with."

"You want dynamite up your ass?" Jorge stood up and slapped a few bills on the bar. As he leaned forward, Jesse saw a holster and gun. "The boss, he makes the decisions. I'll be in touch."

Jesse gave a nod, feeling his pulse hammer at the base of his throat as Jorge stomped out and slammed the door. After a few moments, Jesse got up, relieved the meeting had ended.

Once in his car, Jesse wrapped his hands tight around the steering wheel and let out a sigh of relief mixed with desperate hope. He hated knowing he'd just bet his job on Jorge being able to convince Gonzales to speak to him. As he pulled out of the restaurant's parking lot, he switched on the radio to hear a news flash about Panama.

Sources say Noriega was spotted on the Las Perlas Islands, but no reports have confirmed this. US officials ordered troops to capture the de facto military leader, who they intend to charge with international drug trafficking. With the entire country in turmoil just days before Christmas, it looks like this won't be a very merry holiday season for anyone in this Central American country that has seen much unrest in recent years. . . .

"It's just a pot run to J Street," said Randy.

It was Jesse's 18th birthday, and he and Randy celebrated at the Chicken Coop, a popular Zonian dive bar. The name fit. The dimly-lit open air space had an old wooden bar with a few stools, some plastic tables and chairs, a ratty bathroom and a jukebox. Its charm came from the fact that it sat on the ocean overlooking the Panama Canal. When the jukebox was off, you could hear the waves slapping the shore below.

"That street is dangerous," Jesse told Randy.

"It's not that bad. That's where Sam picks up the merchandise."

"Why don't you have Sam pick it up, then?"

"He's out with some chick, and I'm his partner now, remember?" asked Randy.

Jesse wanted to forget that.

"Okay, I'll take you, but nothing better happen to my car."

Jesse's dad had just given him his pride and joy—a 1967 convertible MG.

"Trust me. In and out," Randy assured him.

Although Jesse had traveled the bad parts of Panama City many times, they usually just drove through for the thrill of it. Going to stop for a purpose would be a first. Jesse felt nervous, despite the kamikaze he had just downed in honor of his birthday.

"This pot is supposed to be great," said Randy, who lit a cigarette and then rolled down the window as they entered the barrio.

"I would hope so," said Jesse. "Don't get ashes in my car."

A couple of minutes later, Randy pointed to a bodega butted up against a tired wooden building that appeared to be almost leaning.

"Holy shit, you're going in there? You want me to come?"

Randy hesitated and then shrugged and hopped out of the MG. "I'm cool. Keep the car running. Back in a flash."

Jesse watched his friend disappear into the dimly lit building; then jerked when a hand touched his arm. A hooker in a tight, pink mini-skirt and neon-green bathing suit top leaned over, filling his car with the odor of sweat and desperation.

"*Quieres jugar, mi amor?*" she asked him in Spanish.

Jesse decided to play dumb. "No speak Spanish."

"*Está bien, no necesitas hablar español,*" she said as she reached down toward his crotch.

Jesse jumped and pulled her hand away; then cupped his privates. He peered at the door where Randy had disappeared. Dammit, where the hell is he? Just then his friend raced from the building, hopped in the car and yelled, "Drive!"

Jesse floored it, his heart leaping as he saw the prostitute reeling in the rearview mirror and two guys emerge from the building wielding what looked like guns. His suspicions were soon confirmed when he heard gunshots chasing them.

Once safely back in the Canal Zone, Jesse pulled to the side of the road and turned to Randy, the volcano of rage he'd kept bottled up finally erupting.

"What the hell was that all about? You trying to get us killed?"

"They're crazy, man. It was nothing," insisted Randy.

"It was something. They shot at us!"

"The guy was a *cholo*. He said I didn't have enough money."

"This is getting totally out of hand," cried Jesse. "I swear, Randy, this is the last time I'm making a run with you. Stop this shit!"

Back home after his meeting with Jorge, Jesse trudged up the steps to his condo and let himself in. Suddenly flattened by fatigue, the bedroom looked to be miles away, so he threw himself onto the couch and fell asleep almost immediately.

Several hours later, Jesse awoke with a start at a pounding sound. Struggling to pull himself out of the cloying effects of a deep sleep, he blinked to focus his eyes and heard his name.

"Jesse, I saw your car. I know you're in there! It's time to party! C'mon, man, open the friggin' door!"

Stumbling to a standing position, Jesse realized it was Micky at the door. He pulled it open; surprised that night had fallen while he slept.

"*Chuleta*," Micky uttered the Panamanian colloquialism used by Zonians that actually meant pork chops. "What the hell happened to you?"

"I did an all-nighter. I'm beat."

"There was a party? Where? I can't believe I missed it."

"No party. I worked for almost thirty hours straight."

"Then you definitely earned some fun tonight," said his friend, pushing his way into Jesse's condo. "There's a killer Zonie party in Fullerton. You gotta go. I heard there's going to be some new people from the Zone. We might meet up with someone we haven't seen in a long time."

Jesse shook his head and started to protest, but Micky stopped him.

"C'mon, man, just for a little while. You're not still on deadline, are you?"

"No, I have a little break," said Jesse. "You might be interested to know that the story I wrote last night was about the Zone and what's going on there. I even talked to your dad."

Micky's bushy, brown eyebrows shot up. "Cool, I can't wait to see what my old man said. I gotta call him. He and my mom okay?"

"Your parents are fine, although your dad dug a bullet out of the side of his house the other night, so calling him would probably be a good idea."

"Man, how far the Zone has fallen, huh? Glad they're okay. Now regarding tonight, you're going. No arguments. You got a mirror around here somewhere?"

"Why do you need a mirror?" asked Jesse. "Not to cut any lines of coke! I told you I don't want that shit in my house."

"Whoa, hold on, man!" Micky threw up his arms, which caused the Van Halen T-shirt he wore to expose his hairy stomach. "I just want to check out my eyes."

"Check out your eyes? Since when are you into primping?"

"Since I started dating this chick named Bridgette, and she's kind of against pot."

"So why the hell did you smoke a joint before you came over?"

"Shit, you can tell? Where the hell is a mirror, for crying out loud?"

"In my bedroom where I get myself all dolled up," said Jesse, following his friend into the back of the condo. "She must not be a Zonian if she doesn't like pot."

"No, but she goes to the parties with a Zonian friend of hers, Ashley Taylor, remember her? Big boobs and black hair?"

Jesse shook his head. "No, maybe you can introduce me to them."

"Who, the girls?"

Jesse laughed. "Yeah, the girls, Micky."

"You sure I don't look stoned?" said Micky as he peered into the mirror over Jesse's bureau.

"You must have it bad," said Jesse. "But looking stoned isn't the problem."

"What do you mean?"

"Your mouth."

"What the fuck's wrong with my mouth?" Micky leaned closer to the mirror and pulled back his lips to eye his slightly buck teeth.

"I'm talking about what's coming out of your mouth. Every other word is a cuss word. And the politically correct term is women, not girls."

"I give the fuck up. Just get dressed for the party," Micky yelled over his shoulder as he headed back to the living room. "You bailed on me last time, so I refuse to take no for an answer."

Jesse sighed. It looked like he'd be going to another Zonian party—to mingle with transplants, who would talk about the good old days in the Zone. Jesse used to go to the parties hoping to run into someone he recognized, but instead he saw people he'd barely known. As the night wore on and many of the partygoers became drunk and stoned, an odd thing happened. All of Jesse's distant acquaintances began reminiscing about the great times they'd had with him. He'd simply nod in agreement when they put a sloppy arm around his shoulder and shared with anyone who would listen about their escapades in the Zone.

After a few hopeful visits to parties as a California newcomer, Jesse realized that what he looked for didn't exist. No matter how many parties he went to, he wouldn't walk into the Chicken Coop and see Lorraine and Randy at the bar. They wouldn't flag him over and buy him a rum and Coke. As a result, he often left the parties disappointed and depressed. He did find Micky to be a hoot, though, and he had turned down the last couple of invitations from him. So, Jesse decided to try to have some fun.

When they headed out a few minutes later, Jesse pulled out his car keys. "I'll drive. It'll give you more time to primp."

Micky directed him to a two-story tract home in a quiet Fullerton neighborhood, where he parked his MG. "Not the typical loud party house you usually drag me to. You must be moving up in the world. Or is it Bridgette's influence?" asked Jesse.

Micky ignored Jesse and headed up the front walkway. Trailing him, Jesse suddenly felt hungry and realized that he hadn't eaten for hours. He hoped there would be more than the usual glop of bean dip and bag of tortilla strips. Micky pushed open the front door of the house to sounds of laughter and the Eagles playing on the stereo. As his friend went in search of Bridgette, Jesse headed straight for the smell of baked bread. To his delight, he found a table in the dining room full of pizza boxes. Sliding two pepperoni and onion slices out of a box and onto a paper plate, Jesse chowed down right where he stood.

"Jesse, Randy's embarrassing me," Lorraine had hissed under her breath one night as the three of them sat in the Canal Zone's Balboa Cafeteria pigging out on burgers and fries after smoking a joint in the jungle.

Randy had been partying for hours, which explained why he didn't notice the catsup dripping down the front of his shirt.

"I swear Jesse, if someone I know sees me. I'll—" gasped Lorraine, sliding her willowy body down into her seat.

"I know. You'll die of mortification. What do you want me to do? Tie a bib around his neck and feed him?"

"Just do something—anything."

"Lorraine's right. You're a mess." Jesse handed his friend a stack of napkins.

"Sorry for being so out of it guys," Randy apologized as he attempted to clean himself up.

"It happens," said Jesse.

"Only to idiots," Lorraine muttered. "What are you going to do with him when we take him home?"

"Put him in the hammock in his backyard."

"You're kidding!" She tossed her head back and laughed for the first time since they arrived at the cafeteria.

"No, that's what I always do. He might be almost a foot shorter than me, but he's dead weight, and I can't get him up the stairs. Besides, I'm not going to explain his condition to his parents."

"That's encouraging. I thought you did everything for him."

"Randy's always there for me. I love him like a brother. Remember the time he covered for us with Old Lady Pritchard's window? If she found out it was really us who broke it, our parents would have canceled our trip to the States. He was on restriction for a month, and he didn't have anything to do with it."

"I know. I love him, too," Lorraine said and sighed. "He just drives me crazy sometimes. He has always been nuts—even when we were little kids."

"Wait, who's nuts?" asked Randy, looking up from the fries he'd been shoveling down.

"No one," said Lorraine and Jesse in unison, both yelling "jinx," which started a laughing fit amongst the three of them that lasted a good five minutes.

Jesse had eaten four pieces of pizza and reached for a fifth when Micky came up to him.

"You won't in a million years believe who I found! Stay right here."

Great, thought Jesse, who had forgotten to warn Micky against putting him through the torture of meeting barely recognizable "old friends." He stood facing the pizza table about ready to bite into another slice when he heard her unmistakable laugh and the voice he'd know anywhere. "I see things haven't changed much," she said. "As usual filling up that hollow leg."

3

Jesse dropped his plate back onto the table and turned around. She stood there smiling, like a cameo shot from some movie. It was as if everything suddenly went silent—as if he could no longer hear. He prayed he didn't look like some kind of fool and struggled to think of something to say as he took in the sight of her. Her face was leaner; high, sharp cheekbones offset by full, soft lips that needed nothing more. The same green eyes, bright and intelligent, and the same laughter, throaty and intimate, that still made him melt. She wore an emerald green sweater that hugged her breasts, jean leggings and the large, silver hoop earrings he remembered as her signature.

"Clare! Is it really you?"

"The last I checked." Clare laughed again and walked into his embrace. Jesse took advantage of the hug, inhaling her familiar vanilla essence. When they finally pulled apart, his hands slid over her silken auburn hair that cascaded down her back, bringing back memories that tangled up his tongue.

"You look great, Jesse," Clare said as she took both of his hands in hers.

"You look better than great," Jesse managed to reply, unable to take his eyes from her. She seemed as self-assured as he remembered, yet wiser and even more confident.

"So, what—?" They both started to talk at once.

Jesse gestured toward a couch in a corner of the room. Taking one of her hands, he led her there and they sat down. A million questions filled his mind, yet he had no idea where to start.

"I never expected to see you here," Clare said.

"You're not the only one. Clare Stinson." Jesse looked at her, shaking his head in wonder. "Is it still Stinson?" He watched her face, waiting for the answer.

"Yes, how about you?" She raised an eyebrow.

Jesse smiled. "Still unhitched. What brings you to Southern California? Or do you live here?"

"I lived in Monterey for eight years but took a job here five months ago."

"What do you do?" Jesse asked, his brain stuck on the fact that she'd lived here for five months. Why hadn't he known that?

"Environmental management."

"That sounds interesting," he said, not wanting to show his ignorance by asking exactly what that entailed.

"It is. What about you? Life been good to you?" Her eyes searched his face.

He nodded. "I'm an investigative reporter for the *LA Times.*"

Clare brightened. "Jesse, how exciting! Do you like it?"

"Love it."

"I'm so happy to hear that." Clare said. She hesitated, and Jesse feared what she might say next.

"It seems like so long ago that we last saw each other, and I guess it really was another lifetime," she said.

Jesse thought of that last night and changed the subject. "So, do you live around here?"

"Yes, I almost gave up the search, but I finally found a great condo in Fullerton with a patio big enough for my plants."

"I live in a condo in Irvine. No plants, but I have a cat." He laughed. "Her name is Millicent."

"I adore cats. How long have you had her?"

"About five years now. Why don't you come over and meet her one night? I'll cook you dinner."

"I would like to. I—" Clare looked up as a short, muscular guy walked up and stopped in front of them.

"Bob, there you are," said Clare. "This is an old friend of mine from the Canal Zone, Jesse McMillan. I haven't seen him in years."

"Great to meet you." Bob flashed one of those overly whitened tooth-paste commercial smiles. "Panama sounds like a great place."

"The best place, but I'm sure Clare told you all about it," said Jesse.

"A little, but I'm more into what's happening now and focusing on the future."

Bob's comment left nothing for anyone to say. Clare finally broke the silence and asked her date, "Want to get going?"

"If you don't mind. I've got a match in the morning with Tom."

"Tennis?" Jesse asked.

"Racquetball."

"Of course, great game," Jesse said.

"Wonderful to see you, Jesse," said Clare over her shoulder as Bob threw an arm around her waist and led her away.

"Even better to see you, Clare, and good luck with your racquetball match," Jesse called after Bob, who didn't turn around, but raised a hand and waved as they made their exit.

As if he'd dreamed the encounter, Clare disappeared. Whenever she left Jesse, Clare had a way of creating a void that made everything suddenly seem boring and mundane.

Jesse had met Clare on an especially muggy day on the Causeway. He, Lorraine and Randy were arguing over who threw the best Frisbee, when Clare drove up with Randy's girl, Missy Blake.

"Hey, there's Missy," Randy said, forgetting about the Frisbee debate.

When the two girls alighted from Missy's car, Lorraine's eyes narrowed as they always did when in the vicinity of another pretty girl. "Who's she with?"

"No idea," Randy replied and shrugged. "I wonder if Missy has any cigs? I'm all out."

Lorraine had reason for apprehension. With the late afternoon sun against her back, the new girl strode toward them on long, tanned legs topped off by turquoise short shorts and a matching spaghetti strap blouse that showed off her shoulders and captured her curves.

"Hi everybody," Missy said as she and her friend approached. "This is Clare. She moved into Fort Clayton last week from Texas. Her dad's in the Army. I told her I would introduce her to the only important crowd in town. This is Randy, my main guy—" Missy said, giving Randy a hug.

"Hey, you mean your only guy!" said Randy. "Got any cigs for him?"

"Don't get technical, and yes, there's some smokes in my purse. Hold your horses. After introductions. This here is Jesse, Randy's best buddy," she said, "And their good friend, Lorraine."

"Nice to meet you," said Jesse, who saw Lorraine cast Clare a guarded smile.

"You girls want a beer?" Randy asked, approaching the red and white cooler sitting beside his VW.

"Sure," Missy replied.

"No thanks," said Clare. "Got any soda?"

"Soda! Who drinks soda?" Randy exclaimed, but Missy quieted him with a warning look.

"I think we're all out, Clare," Jesse said.

That was just the beginning of the radical differences between Clare Stinson and these lifelong Zonians. Clare's political views drew a lot more ire from Randy than her drinking habits. One night several weeks later, Randy, Missy and Jesse debated the likelihood of the rumors being true that the Zone would be given back to the Panamanians. Clare remained silent for a time, and then asked, "How can you expect the Panamanians to put up with your living high on the hog in the middle of their country forever?"

Her words fell like a bowling ball at their feet. Jesse said nothing at first.

True to form, Randy reacted immediately. "What a bogus thing to say, Clare! They're lucky we're here. The Zone gives the Panamanians lots of good jobs. This country would be a pigsty without us. If you don't believe me, take a walk down J Street in Chorrillo."

"They might not see it as luck," Clare said. "And Chorrillo is beside the point. Every area has a slum. LA has Watts. New York has Harlem."

"Look, Clare, this is our home, okay? We don't talk that way around here." Randy turned to Jesse for help, but he only compounded the issue.

"She's got a point," Jesse said.

"What the hell does that mean? You both sound like traitors."

"No, we're not traitors, but it must be hard for them to see us here in our nice houses, when many of them are so poor," said Jesse.

"This conversation's getting way too heavy for me," Randy said. "All I know is, even if they're stupid enough to give the Zone away, I'm never leaving. Ever."

After Clare left the party and his resulting trip down memory lane, Jesse suddenly felt the flattening fatigue of missing a night of sleep. He found Micky in the kitchen sitting on the counter with his legs wrapped around Bridgette's waist.

"Was that totally unreal or what?" asked Micky. "Clare Stinson! I can't believe it. Where'd she go?"

"She went home, and that's where I should go," said Jesse. "I'm beat."

"I'll give him a ride home," Bridgette said, smiling up at Micky.

"Thanks, I appreciate it," Jesse said. "And really nice to meet you."

The next afternoon at work as Jesse read an investigative story about cock fighting written by a rival paper's top reporter, he couldn't help but wonder about Clare. She worked in environmental management. Where?

He thought about how he might locate her, but then what? The phone rang and Jesse grabbed it, hoping for good news from Jorge.

"McMillan here."

"Jesse, it's Clare. I hope you don't mind me calling you. You said you worked at the *Times*, so I called the main number, and the receptionist put me through to you."

"Of course not, Clare. Nice to hear from you."

"I'm sorry about last night at the party. I didn't mean to rush out like that."

"No harm done."

"You mentioned dinner and I—"

"Look, sorry to put you on the spot with, what's his name?"

"Bob."

"I had no idea you were with someone." Although Jesse couldn't imagine why he presumed that. Clare was a beauty. Why wouldn't she be with someone?

"Dinner sounds really nice," said Clare.

That stopped Jesse for a second.

"I don't want to make waves," he said. He'd caused enough trouble for her in high school.

Clare laughed. "I'm a big girl, and I know how to swim."

"As I recall, you swim quite well. I still have visions of that hot pink bikini you wore in Panama." If she wanted to come over, no point in delaying things. "How about my house tonight at seven o'clock?" he asked. "Is that okay?"

"Seven is great," she said. "Give me your address."

Clare coming to his house, Jesse marveled as he hung up a couple of minutes later, only to pick up the receiver again when it rang.

"McMillan here."

"*Amigo.* I talked to *el Jefe*," said Jorge.

"And?"

"He'll meet with you, but you need to prove to him he can trust you."

"What is this, a high school initiation or something?"

"No high school I want my kids at," said Jorge. "Go to Cecilia's diner on First in Santa Ana in half an hour and wait to hear from us."

Jesse hung up the phone. If they thought he would prove himself by doing something that could land him in prison for the next twenty years, they were dead wrong. Without talking to anyone, Jesse sprinted out of the newsroom. If he was going to do this, he didn't want to be late.

Fifteen minutes later, he pulled into the parking lot at Cecilia's diner. When he walked in the door, the smell of fried tortillas and simmering pork tantalized his taste buds momentarily, but the nervous knot in his stomach told him to forget it. Inquisitive eyes followed Jesse as he made his way to an orange vinyl booth next to the window.

A petite, young waitress with a braided bun on top of her head approached Jesse's booth and asked, "Can I help you, Mister?"

"*Quiero café.*"

"Cream and sugar? Do you want a churro? They're fresh."

"Both cream and sugar, and a churro sounds great, thanks," said Jesse, whose mouth watered at the memory of the sweet fried pastry's cinnamony taste.

Three cups of coffee and two churros later, Jesse snorted in frustration and slapped down a ten-dollar bill. As he rose to leave, a hand landed on his shoulder with a grip that told him he wasn't going anywhere.

"*Señor* McMillan?"

Jesse looked up into the face of a Mexican ox, whose broad set eyes warned him to stay seated.

"Yeah."

"Let's take a drive." The ox gripped Jesse's shoulder, guiding him to stand.

The idea of going to the bathroom and then slipping out the window flashed through Jesse's mind, but his messenger had no intention of letting go. The ox guided him outside into the parking lot where a black stretch limo waited. Reaching around to open the door, he shoved Jesse in, which caused his heart to lurch in his chest. As he sat down to face the front of the car, Jesse glimpsed a man in the back of the limo. He wore an overcoat and his face was shadowed by a black fedora hat. Who the hell was that? Jesse's anxiety ratcheted up several notches as the ox slid in next to him. What if Jorge had had it with him and they planned to take him to an empty field and force him to kneel while they blew his brains out?

"I see you found our visitor waiting as instructed," said the voice from the back. "*Señor* Gonzales will be pleased."

"Looked like he almost left," said Jesse's escort.

"Not a wise move." Something about the voice alerted Jesse. Where had he heard it before?

"We're going to take a little tour of some areas important to *Señor* Gonzales," the voice added.

The limo eased into traffic and headed into the heart of downtown Santa Ana. They drove in silence for a time until they hit Minnie Street, a treacherous gang territory the police avoided. Composed of two-story, decrepit apartment buildings, Jesse knew the five-block area to be packed with thousands of poor, mostly illegal immigrants forced to navigate the mean streets where curbside drug deals occurred twenty-four/seven.

"This is the street where *Señor* Gonzales lived for a time. Ever seen anything like this?"

"Yes," said Jesse, remembering el Chorrillo in Panama.

"But you weren't forced to live on such a street, were you? Your street in the Canal Zone was much cleaner than this, much safer," the voice said, as if reading Jesse's mind. "You grew up on a street with palm trees and no litter. No rats. Many of these people would kill for such a life. But then you know about death, don't you *Señor* McMillan?"

"What are you driving at?" Jesse asked, unease slithering across his skin. How and why did this man know so much about him, he wondered? "You seem to be well acquainted with my past."

"Your career must be very exciting. Tell me how you get your sources, *Señor* McMillan."

"I don't talk about my sources."

"Right answer."

"I'd go to jail before revealing a source," said Jesse. "You can tell *Señor*

Gonzales that." He wanted to turn and glance at the man sitting behind him, but thought better of it.

"So, you think you would not mind rotting in jail for a few years, *Señor* McMillan?"

"I would hope it wouldn't come to that, but I stand by my responsibility as a journalist to protect my sources."

The man snickered. "What do you know of jail, *Señor* McMillan? You haven't rotted in a Latin jail, or even spent one night in a much kinder American jail. You haven't slept with one eye open to ensure you aren't knifed, or worse, been forced to debase yourself to survive." The man's voice revealed a bitter edge.

"Maybe I haven't spent time in jail, but good friends have."

"It is wise that you have no wife and children, *Señor* McMillan. Your job isn't conducive to family life."

This comment reminded Jesse of his dinner date with Clare. He looked at his watch—almost six o'clock. She was coming at seven. Agitated at the possibility of standing her up, Jesse blurted, "We almost done here? I have an appointment this evening. Will I be able to see Gonzales?"

"I don't like his tone," said the man, "and I'm sure *Señor* Gonzales would not approve."

"Right," the ox said, grabbing Jesse's hand and bending his fingers backward.

"What the fuck?" Jesse yelled in pain.

"When we speak of *el Jefe*, we must speak respectfully, *Señor* McMillan," said the voice. "Something like, 'May I speak to *Señor* Gonzales, please?'"

"Okay. Okay. May I speak to *Señor* Gonzales, please, *Señor* . . . what is your name? I can't be polite if I don't even know your name."

"Too many questions," the man said. Jesse shouted when the ox bent his fingers back farther.

"We'll talk to *Señor* Gonzales for you, *Señor* McMillan. What message would you like us to give him?"

"Let go of my fucking hand and I'll tell you."

"He's got a big mouth," said the voice, which prompted the henchman to continue the torture until a mixture of fear and pain shut Jesse's brain down momentarily.

"Tell him I don't talk about my sources," Jesse cried. "That I would rot in jail if the Feds or somebody wanted my notes. Shit, let go of my hand!"

"There he goes with that mouth again."

This time Jesse heard a crack and screamed in agony.

"That is nothing compared to what will happen to you if you open your mouth when you're not supposed to, *Señor* McMillan," the man spit the words out as the ox let Jesse's hand drop. "But you are a writer—a man with a creative mind. You can only imagine what else we will do to you."

The limo stopped short at a corner, and the ox opened the door and got out. As he did so, Jesse saw a matchbook on the seat next to him and picked it up with his good hand, tucking it into his pocket.

The ox stood at attention outside of the car while Jesse's unknown host informed him, "I'm afraid we've got other plans now. Sorry we can't drop you off at your car."

Jesse managed to scoot himself out of the limo and steadied himself on the side of the road as the ox got back inside and slammed the door in his face.

He watched the limo speed off into the night, furious with himself that he got into the car in the first place, yet relieved at escaping with only a battered hand. Nothing to do now but walk to his car. Taxis were hard to find in Southern California, and most likely impossible to locate in the barrio. After a grueling half jog that sent intense pain radiating from his hand up through his arm, Jesse arrived at his car thirty minutes later. At 7:30 pm, he finally pulled into his complex and parked, convinced that Clare had come and gone.

He let out a big sigh of relief when he headed to his condo and spied her sitting on the steps. She stood up, immediately sensing that something was wrong.

"Jesse, what happened? Were you in an accident?"

"You could call it that," he said as he approached, drinking in the sight of her in a white angora sweater and long gold skirt. "Sorry about dinner," said Jesse. "I'm kind of out of commission. Want to order pizza?"

"Were you mugged? Should I call the police?"

"No, no police," Jesse said sharply.

"Tell me what happened," she said, gingerly taking the keys from his good hand, while eyeing his broken one with growing concern on her face.

"Occupational health hazard," he moaned as the throbbing in his hand suddenly intensified.

Clare's eyes widened. "This has something to do with your job?"

"It's all right. I've got great benefits. Health insurance. Life insurance," he babbled, holding back tears from the pain and an overwhelming relief that washed over him now that he was home and with Clare.

"You're going to the hospital immediately," she said. "That hand needs treatment. And don't even try to tell me no. I'll drive."

Jesse nodded in agreement, thinking about the welcoming effects of pain meds. As they turned toward Clare's car, his heart jumped into his throat when he saw what looked like the limo turning at an intersection down the street. Did that sadistic bastard follow him to his car and home? The worst part—now he'd seen Clare.

4

The ox had broken Jesse's forefinger and middle finger, and the next morning it felt that way. At the moment his whole hand throbbed. Last night, the emergency room doctor assured Jesse that he'd have full range of motion in two to three months. His only consolation was that they'd broken his left fingers, not his right, so at least he'd still be able to work.

"You're awake," Clare said, coming in and sitting on the side of his bed. "How do you feel?"

The only positive thing in this whole mess, Clare insisted on staying over. She even looked good in yesterday's clothes.

"Like playing the piano. You sleep okay on the couch?" asked Jesse.

"A little lumpy, but I'll survive."

"I sleep on that couch all of the time. It's not lumpy. You're like that princess and the pea," Jesse said, kicking himself for being silly.

Clare smiled at his comment. With her long hair cascading down her back, bare feet and the shimmery gold of her skirt, she looked like an exotic gypsy. Jesse felt suddenly aroused gazing at her and thankful for the blanket covering him.

"I fed your cat. She's a beauty, and what a great disposition she has." The cat rubbed against her leg and she picked it up.

"Thanks for feeding Millicent. As far as a great disposition, that's all an act. She likes you, because you fed her."

Clare threw her head back and laughed that throaty chuckle that always made Jesse want to join in. She placed the cat on the edge of Jesse's bed.

"Do you want another pain pill?" she asked.

"I could use one, but I hate to muddle myself up. I've got some thinking to do."

"Being macho, are we?" she said.

"No, I'm safer sober," he said.

Clare frowned. "Exactly how much danger are you in?"

"More than you're in with Bob after having stayed the night with me."

"Maybe you should just go to the police."

"No police," Jesse said. "This is a big story. They'll just screw things up. And speaking of screwing things up, please don't tell anyone about this, even Bob."

"More than you're screwed up right now? Look at yourself. And of course, I won't tell anyone."

"Promise me, Clare. Maybe you and Bob tell each other everything, but not this," said Jesse.

"Bob and I don't do much talking," Clare said, and then reddened. "All I mean is. . . . He's just not that talkative."

Jesse laughed. "You mean he likes to talk about Bob, and Bob is kind of boring?"

Clare sat silent for a moment and then replied, "He's a nice guy when you get to know him."

"That's what they all say," said Jesse, quickly adding, "Sorry, it's none of my business. I really do appreciate you helping me. All this pain and drama has suddenly given me an appetite. Would you mind getting me a bowl of cereal or something?"

After he finished eating breakfast, the throbbing in Jesse's hand intensified, so he gave in and asked Clare for a pain pill. As he began dozing off awhile later, she whispered in his ear, "I have to get to a cleanup site. I'll put the TV on for you."

He remembered wishing she would just strip and climb into bed with him. He hoped he hadn't said it out loud.

An hour later, the sound of the gardener blowing leaves outside woke Jesse. Easing himself up in bed with his good hand, he focused his attention on the television set that droned on across the room.

"Unsubstantiated reports have placed Noriega at Cristóbal, a port town on the Atlantic side of the Panama Canal. Conditions continue to worsen in this once peaceful Latin American country," said the foreign correspondent, standing in relative safety in front of the old Panama Canal Administration Building in Balboa Heights. The television station followed his report with shots of downtown Panama. Rioters and those caught in the crossfire ran through the streets like mice in a broken-down maze.

Many of Jesse's Zonian friends, like Micky, had an I-told-you-so attitude about the unrest brewing in Panama for the last few years, insisting that the Panamanians knew nothing about running their own country, but Jesse knew things couldn't be explained away so easily. The current unrest came from Noriega's tyrannical rule. Viewing the newly bred chaos in the once serene country made Jesse grateful for the first time since he'd left not to be there. He found it difficult enough to watch the destruction on television. It would break his heart to see it firsthand. And he had to admit that California had grown on him. At least as a US citizen, he was technically home, even if he considered Panama his first home. He thought about how Panamanians weren't so lucky—like his good friend Pablo Sanchez. Where was Pablo now, he wondered? They kept track of each other for a few years after Jesse and his family had left the Zone, but it'd been a long time since he'd heard from Pablo, who had given him insight into what it meant to be a Panamanian.

"So many *chicas* to choose from, no?" said Pablo as they watched girls dance to the T-Bird band at the Canal Zone Yacht Club.

Jesse nodded and chewed on a meaty empanada.

Adjusting the gold chain around his neck, Pablo reached into the pocket of his black silk shirt for a packet of cigarettes. Gripping a Marlboro between his teeth, he searched for a lighter, but Jesse beat him to it and handed him his.

Pablo always appeared so cool and measured, like his father, a high-ranking official in the Panamanian government. Jesse often wondered if his friend was privy to any top secrets. Did he know the inside scoop on the treaty? Jesse wished someone would give him a straight answer about whether the treaties would be signed. He wanted to go back to feeling secure in his home—not all jostled up inside, constantly waiting and dreading news.

That wasn't Jesse's only problem. Lorraine was dancing with Ricardo Montego again, instead of with him. She smiled as she wiggled to the beat of La Bamba.

"They are dating?" Pablo asked, gesturing to the dance floor.

"I don't know." Jesse shrugged his shoulders and turned his attention away from Lorraine.

"Ricardo is no good. He's a *maliante*—a bad boy. He only seeks one thing," Pablo said.

"I'm not her keeper."

"You gringos, *que loco*."

Jesse looked at Pablo and his strong jawline as he sucked on his cigarette and then exhaled. What would Pablo do in this situation? Grab Lorraine and tell her, I don't want you with him, you're my *chica*. Jesse could never do that, but Pablo saw it as a matter of pride. On many occasions, Pablo had tried to explain Panamanian honor to Jesse, while Jesse had countered by relating his way of looking at things—not showing your hand unless you have to. That meant never pulling Lorraine off the dance floor, even when she danced with an asshole. He and Pablo could never understand one another on the subject. While ignoring the situation saved Jesse's pride, it would have killed Pablo's.

"American *chicas* are like the wild horses in Panama's untamed Interior," said Pablo, breaking the silence. "They kick and bite and run before they find out that you are there to feed them. They refuse to be caged.

Too rough-spirited. Why don't you find yourself a Panamanian girl? They talk a lot, but they are not so wild."

"Right now, I like Lorraine," said Jesse.

"It's your life." Pablo shook his head as he exhaled.

"What about you. You have a girl?"

Pablo hesitated. "There are so many *chicas*, but yes, one has taken my heart."

"Who? Do I know her?" asked Jesse.

"No, her father is an *oficial* in another country."

"Do you ever see her?" Jesse wanted to know.

"Not much," said Pablo.

"Can't you go visit?"

"It is political. It has to do with relations between the governments of our countries. I am not really supposed to see her."

"See her anyway," said Jesse.

"It's not that easy. You *Americanos* think everything is so easy, because you can move around as you wish. We Panamanians are not so lucky," said Pablo.

Jesse pulled his attention back to the television to hear some political analysts discussing Noriega's many years of drug running and the people in power he was suspected of murdering. He looked at his hand and thought of Gonzales. Was this it now? Broken fingers and nothing to show for his pain? As if on cue, the phone rang.

"McMillan here," he answered.

"I understand you had a small tour last night," said Jorge.

"Do you also understand the bastard broke my fingers? What the hell is going on?"

"I told you this is serious shit, *amigo*."

"I figured that out last night. Tell me my next tour, as you call it, won't break my legs."

"The boss doesn't want to get a bad reputation for hurting journalists. He just had to get the point across as to what happens if you cross us."

"Message received loud and clear," Jesse assured him. "Now what?"

"Now you wait to hear from me. I'll give the word when you can meet the boss."

"So, he has agreed to see me?" Jesse asked, trying not to let too much hopeful relief creep into his tone.

"It looks that way right now."

"Is that code for he might change his mind?" Jesse felt some of the relief evaporate.

"Shit happens when you run an organization this major, and we're just about on top of Christmas, but he'll most likely be available. I'll let you know when and where."

"Look, Jorge, call me *loco*, but I'm nervous."

"I told you. He's giving you access," Jorge assured him. "You'll be fine. Gonzales wants to talk."

"Okay, but this time, I want to meet at Hotel Miramar near the airport. The newspaper has an account there. I will get a suite."

Jorge hesitated. "He might agree to that if I can get him in through the back, and I go in and sweep first."

"Of course," said Jesse. "I wouldn't have it any other way."

"I'll call you soon with a day and time."

"Thanks, Jorge," said Jesse.

"Yeah, gringo. Just stick to your end of the bargain. *El Jefe* wants to be quoted accurately. You come alone and absolutely no photos. *Comprende?*"

"I got it," said Jesse, but Jorge had already hung up the phone.

"Cross your paws that I can keep you living in the style you've become accustomed to," Jesse said to Millicent when she hopped up onto his lap. "It's looking like Gonzales might actually talk to me."

Just as he said this, a worrisome thought popped into Jesse's mind. Why all of a sudden had it been so easy? What was Gonzales's game here, and would that game be Russian roulette with Jesse on the receiving end of a chance bullet?

5

By midafternoon, Jesse decided he'd better make an appearance at the paper. He dreaded explaining his hand to Burt, but no point in delaying the inevitable.

Getting himself ready proved difficult. In the bathroom, he gazed into the mirror at the dark shadows under his eyes, like upturned crescents. A two-day stubble covered the lower half of his face, but mustering up the energy to lather up and wield the razor with one hand seemed like way too much work. Maybe a trendy bit of beard would add something to his persona when meeting with Gonzales. Make him appear older, tougher, and not so clean-cut.

After doing a one-handed dance to put on his pants and getting stuck in his shirt for a time as he struggled to pull it over his head, he finally managed to dress and get out the door.

Pulling into the *Times'* parking lot a few minutes later, Jesse took the first available space and walked into the building's main entryway to be greeted by Juan, head of maintenance, who stood talking to a window cleaner about the state of the room's floor-to-ceiling windows.

"Jesse, *mi amigo, qué pasa!*" said the short, balding man.

"Juan, *mi amigo, qué pasa contigo?* Looks like you're keeping things in order around here. The Christmas tree looks great," Jesse said, referring to the ten-foot-tall tree that graced the corner of the lobby.

"Of course, Juan's the big *hombre* around here." The old man grinned. "You find a nice *esposa* yet?"

"No wife yet," said Jesse, who knew what came next. During his rounds, Juan scouted out single women in the building and reported back to Jesse. Each time, he prefaced his suggestions with the same patter. "You are almost thirty years old Jesse, truth? At thirty, I had three *niños*. In accounting yesterday, I saw this wonderful *chiquita*. Her name is Mary. Beautiful, huh?" Juan grinned. "You know Mary?"

"No, but maybe she'll give me a raise on my next paycheck. Gotta get to work. Deadlines," Jesse said, hopping into the elevator.

"I bet she is a good cook," Juan called after him. "When you get to my age, these things are important."

Jesse chuckled to himself and pushed the button for the fourth floor. As he waited for the elevator to make its ascent, he reached into his pocket and found the matchbook he'd picked up in the limo. It was from a place called La Estrella Bar & Grill.

When the elevator stopped and Jesse exited, he ran straight into Phil, who stood waiting to get on.

"Sorry," Jesse muttered, taking in a sharp breath as the impact shot pain to his wounded fingers.

"Hey, no problem. I'm off to pose as a baseball fan, even though I think the game's boring," Phil said, getting into the elevator, but not before taking notice of Jesse's casted hand. "Burt wants me to do a big series on sports nuts—how far they'll go for their sport and all that. What happened to your hand? I know it's not from too much writing." He snorted a laugh as the elevator doors closed.

Jesse made his way through the maze of desks to the center of the newsroom and sat down, deciding to check his phone messages before getting to work. He stopped when he caught sight of Burt standing in the doorway of his office with a "get in here, and I mean now" expression that got Jesse out of his chair immediately.

"What happened, and I want the truth. No imaginary heroics," Burt demanded as Jesse eased himself into a chair while his boss closed the door to his office.

"Gonzales's men gave me a warning."

"Why?"

"They wanted me to get the message that protecting my sources is important."

"I'd call this a message all right," grunted Burt. "I thought I told you not to get hurt?"

"Actually, you told me not to get killed. I'm okay, boss."

"Okay? Look at you. You're a mess. And next time it could be dead instead of hurt. It pains me to say this, but maybe you should hang this one up."

Jesse leaned toward Burt. "I can't. I've finally got him. Gonzales agreed to the story. It's going to work out."

Burt gave Jesse a long, measured look and finally said, "Damn it all."

He watched the struggle in his boss's face. Despite eighteen years of editing at one of the nation's top newspapers, Burt still didn't have a writer with a Pulitzer. He wanted it almost as bad as Jesse, but a dead reporter would ruin his career.

Burt strummed the fingers of one hand on a scarce open space on his desk while Jesse waited, half holding his breath, afraid of what might come next. Finally, his boss sighed and asked, "You want this McMillan, don't you?"

"As the old cliché goes, so bad I can taste it."

"To use another cliché, I sure as shit hope I don't regret this. Finish the damn story."

"Thanks, boss," Jesse said. When he got back to his desk, he thumbed through his business card file and dialed the number of a reporter he'd met a few months back.

"Alexa Kent speaking."

"Hi, my name is Jesse McMillan. I'm with the *Times*. We talked at a press club meeting last September."

"Sure, I remember. What's up?"

"I'm looking for information on a place called La Estrella Bar & Grill."

"Just about the biggest Mexican mafia hangout in Southern California," she said.

"What else can you tell me about it?" asked Jesse, recalling that Alexa worked at the *San Diego Union Tribune* as a Latin America foreign correspondent.

"It's not surprising, but most people are close-mouthed there."

"Most people?"

"There are a few cocktail waitresses who talk now and then, especially to good looking guys—if you grease their palms."

"Can you give me any names in particular?" asked Jesse.

Alexa hesitated and then said, "I think I have a good lead for you."

"I guess that means I pass the test?"

"What test?" she asked.

"I'm good looking enough for the cocktail waitresses to talk to me?"

Alexa laughed. "You'll do just fine. There's one waitress in particular with pretty loose lips. Her name's Ginger."

"For extra insurance, I can take along a muscle-bound construction buddy," offered Jesse.

"Even better," said Alexa.

Moments after Jesse hung up, the phone rang.

"McMillan here."

"Hi, it's Clare."

"How's it going?"

"Great. How's your hand?"

"Not great, but bearable. What's up?"

"We had a sale at the bio intensive farm yesterday, and I have some extra plants. Want me to make a few container gardens for your patio?"

"Sure," replied Jesse, hoping that no one saw the goofy grin plastered on his face at the prospect of seeing Clare again. "But I can't help much with this hand."

"No problem. I can do the planting this Saturday, if you want."

"Look, is this going to cause any trouble with Bob?"

"It's no problem. He can't object to me visiting an old friend. And besides, I do what I want."

"You always have," said Jesse, hanging up the phone and smiling. Back in Panama, Clare always did what she wanted, when she wanted, without worrying about everyone else's opinion—unlike Lorraine, who refused to choose nail polish without wondering what the entire student body would think.

"Where's Lorraine?" asked Randy's girl, Missy, one night when she met up with the gang at the Chicken Coop.

"We were having a great time telling jokes and drinking rum and Cokes, but she disappeared when I went to the bathroom," said Jesse.

"Maybe she went to the bathroom, too," Missy offered.

Randy came up behind them. "She's not in the bathroom. She's talking to that *cholo*, Ricardo. What is her fascination with that creep?"

"She thinks kissing up to Ricardo will get her some modeling jobs," said Missy. "His mom owns Hermosa Modeling Agency downtown. She also likes how he treats her like a lady. He always lights her cigarettes and opens car doors for her. He even pulls out chairs before she sits down."

"I didn't know she was such an invalid," said Randy. "Maybe he'll get her a wheelchair."

"She can marry the asshole, for all I care," said Jesse, downing the rest of his rum and Coke in one long swallow. "Have a bunch of *cholo* babies."

Clare appeared at the bar. "Who's having a bunch of *cholo* babies?" she asked.

"No one," said Jesse, giving Missy and Randy a warning look.

To hell with Lorraine, Jesse thought. He might have crushed on her since grade school, but she apparently liked Ricardo now. Clare, the new girl, stood there looking as sensational as ever in a blue tank top and matching shorts that accented all the right curves. Clearly a sign for Jesse to move on.

"Sit down," he patted the bar stool next to him.

Clare's long, auburn hair brushed up against Jesse's arm as she climbed onto the stool, sending a pleasant rush of warmth throughout his body that he knew didn't come from the rum and Cokes.

"You want something to drink?"

"What are you having?" asked Clare.

"Rum and Coke," said Jesse.

"I'll have the same."

"Hey, guys, me and Missy are going for a ride. Alone if you don't mind," announced Randy, who took his girlfriend by the hand.

"No problem," said Jesse. "Clare knows I don't bite."

Clare giggled, and called after them, "Go ahead, you two love birds."

Now Jesse wished he hadn't had so many drinks. He didn't want to sound stupid with Clare, who seemed really together.

"You like living in the Zone so far?" he asked after Randy and Missy left.

"It's definitely different from the last couple of places I lived."

"Where'd you live before?"

"Texas and before that California."

"Is it nice in California?" Jesse asked. "My Aunt Marge lives there, but I've only been once as a kid."

"Yeah, it's really nice. I love everything about it—the beaches, mountains, warm weather."

"I love it *here*," said Jesse.

"I can tell that a lot of people do."

A comfortable silence hung in the air between them for a while and then Jesse suggested they go for a ride to the jungle.

Once in Jesse's MG, Clare ran her hand over the dashboard and commented, "This car is really nice."

"Thanks. It used to be my dad's, but it's mine now."

When he and his friends craved an experience with a little more edge to it, something out of the ordinary, they went to the jungle. Since childhood, Jesse had heard enough stories to maintain a healthy respect for what the locals called *la selva*—endless miles of green. He loved standing in the cool, dense growth in the middle of the day and gazing up at the towering canopy of trees, searching for the sun. He rarely saw it, but rays of light did occasionally sneak in and disappear. Beneath his feet, the jungle carpeting lay spongy with leaf litter, and the sound of the millions of insects that inhabited the tropical forest reached a crescendo built on syncopated rhythms, like nothing else on earth. Sometimes the sound grew so loud Jesse wished for earplugs. There, in the lush growth, the air hung so thick with humidity that he often saw his own breath.

"Wow, it's dark," said Clare as they traveled through the jungle town of Gamboa, which they would have passed without noticing, if not for the occasional light in a window. Once they left the town limits, the brilliant splash of stars across the sky provided the only real light. Jesse pulled off the road and slowed down, the MG bumping up and down on the spongy earth. A few feet in front of them, the headlights slit the darkness. When a thick-trunked tree sprang up in front of them, Jesse knew they had reached the jungle's edge, so he braked and turned off the car.

"It's so dark out here, Jesse," said Clare as the world in front of them became inky black. "Even though I can't see the trees, I feel them."

"That's the best part," said Jesse. "The trees are so massive; it makes me lightheaded to think about it. But not too lightheaded to smoke a joint. Want to?"

Clare nodded.

Jesse reached over to open the glove compartment and felt around for a cigarette holder that contained a joint and a lighter. Pulling it out, he lit up and took a toke, then passed it to Clare. She sucked in deeply and passed it back.

"You smoke pot in Texas?"

"Yeah, a little."

"Panama Red is the best," said Jesse, taking another toke.

"I've never been out here in the jungle at night," said Clare. "I like it. With my dad in the service, I've been to a lot of cool places in the world, but this tops the list. The buzzing is insects, right?" she said of the low hum coming from the jungle.

"Yeah, a ton of them," said Jesse. "Our science teacher said there are some insects in there we haven't even discovered yet. And I don't know if this is going to affect your feelings about the place, but it trips me out to think that there are thirty-foot boa constrictors hanging from trees just yards away."

"I know. I read about them. I'd love to see one sometime." Clare laughed. "But probably not tonight."

"Maybe a day trip," said Jesse, impressed with Clare's no-fear attitude. As high as he felt, it was no time to be stumbling around in the jungle trying to impress her.

After finishing the joint, the two talked for a couple of hours—about the jungle, the Zone, the States and going to college. How easily they related amazed Jesse. They moved from one subject to another without any awkward silences. And even more incredible, they agreed on so many things, like how they both hated algebra, but loved English and planned on going to big colleges. Both only children, they also agreed they found it far from lonely, since they got a lot of attention from their parents and could always visit friends with siblings and then go home to a quiet house. Finally, Clare looked at her watch and yawned.

"I'm supposed to be home by midnight," she said. "Can you take me? Missy drove tonight, and who knows where she is now."

"Sure," Jesse said, starting the car and heading towards Fort Clayton, an Army base a few miles from the yacht club. When they got to her house, he pulled up behind an RV on the street.

"Is that your parents'?" he asked.

"Yeah, it's neat. My dad just bought it so we can go camping in the Interior. Want to see inside?"

"You sure it's okay?"

"We'll be quiet."

Jesse followed Clare up the RV's metal steps.

"Cool," he said, when they stepped into a kitchen-living room area. He looked at the back of the RV. "Do you sleep back there?"

Clare took Jesse by the hand, guiding him along a narrow passageway. She stopped and turned around, a smile playing at the corners of her mouth. Should he kiss her? Jesse wondered. He wanted to. As he thought about how to pull the kiss off, in one fluid movement Clare met his mouth with hers. Her lips were soft and open, as if yearning for the feel of his tongue on hers. Jesse placed one hand on her breast as they kissed, expecting her to push him away. Instead, she moaned, and together they unbuttoned her blouse, and she guided Jesse to unclip her bra. He marveled at the softness of her breasts and the sweet smell of her skin. After a couple of minutes of kissing that all but numbed Jesse's brain, she led him through a small open doorway and sat down on the bed of the RV, looking up at him as she removed her blouse and bra.

"Are you sure about this?" Jesse asked. When she nodded and lay back, he slid off her shorts and silk panties and pulled off his clothes, kicking them to one side. Meeting her welcoming eyes as he eased on top of her, Jesse thought this wasn't how he imagined his first time would be—it was a million times better.

6

Jesse walked through the mall, willing himself to concentrate on the Christmas music wafting through the air, rather than on the fact that Jorge still hadn't called. When he got home earlier from the paper, he tried lounging in his recliner and watching television, but the Christmas commercials reminded him that the year before he showed up at his parents' house on Christmas Day without any presents, because he'd been on deadline. He wanted to give them something this year, and shopping would get his mind off Jorge's call.

At the kitchen store he found the perfect gift for his mom, who loved to cook. A large serving platter decorated with one of her favorite sayings —Home, Sweet Home. For his dad, a beer lover, he got a beer making kit. They could try getting a batch started when he went over to celebrate the holiday.

That done, Jesse's thoughts turned to Clare. Should he get her something? And if so, what? As if an answer to his question, he spotted a jewelry store. Maybe something simple, he thought, entering to find a well-dressed, middle-aged man behind the jewelry counter.

"Happy holidays, and how may I help you?" he asked Jesse.

"I'm not sure."

"Buying for your wife, girlfriend, lady friend?" When Jesse didn't answer, he added, "Your mother? Grandmother?"

"A lady friend. I've never really done this before, so I'm not sure what would be appropriate."

"How close are you and your lady friend?"

Another tough question, thought Jesse. "We've known each other for a long time, but are just recently getting reacquainted," he answered.

"And the lady's taste? Subdued, elegant? Or does she have a bit of flair?"

"I'd go with elegant, but not stuffy," said Jesse.

The man pulled a keychain from his pocket, unlocking the jewelry case on his side. With thin, nimble fingers, he reached in and extracted a bracelet that he handed to Jesse.

Splayed out in Jesse's palm, the brushed sterling silver bracelet appeared to have small blue blossoms woven into the chain.

"Those are violets," said the salesman. "Quite delicate and understated, but gorgeous."

"She loves plants."

The man beamed a smile. "Then this is a splendid choice."

"I'll take it," said Jesse.

"You don't wish to look at more options?" the salesman asked.

Jesse shook his head. "No, I'm a quick shopper, and I know that it fits her perfectly."

"Well then, it sounds like you know your lady friend quite well."

Jesse smiled, imagining the bracelet on Clare's wrist.

By the time he got back to his complex, his daydreams about Clare had progressed to her thanking him in a very pleasant way for the bracelet. When he approached his condo and heard the phone ringing, he ran up the steps, hoping for Clare on the other end of the line. What did they say? Ask the universe, and the universe delivered? Hopefully he'd be that lucky!

After fumbling with the key in the lock and throwing the door open, he thought he might miss the call, but managed to pick it up mid-ring and gasped into the phone, "Hello?"

"Hope I'm interrupting something, and you finally got a piece of ass, *amigo*."

"Jorge?"

"Who the fuck else?"

"Where are you? I can barely hear you."

"A strip joint downtown. Some business with the owner. The view ain't bad, though."

"You have some good news, I hope," Jesse said, sitting down to catch his breath.

"Yeah, *el Jefe* wants to talk tomorrow. The Hotel Miramar will fly. We'll get a suite."

"No offense, Jorge, but the paper can foot the bill for this one. I'll leave the room number at the front desk. What time is good for him tomorrow?"

"*Mierda, gringo*, you're lucky I like you. Okay, two o'clock in the afternoon."

The next day Jesse arrived an hour early for his meeting with Gonzales. No such thing as too cautious, he thought, scanning the lobby. He knew Jorge respected his ballsy behavior, but he also knew that if given the order, the enforcer wouldn't hesitate about disposing of Jesse.

The hotel gave him a corner suite with a large sitting area featuring rich, leather furniture and contemporary geometric art lining the walls. A large black vase filled with red anthuriums graced the coffee table. Checking out the room, Jesse noted that the window opened onto hedges below. He'd chosen this particular second story suite, so that he could drop to safety, if necessary—providing he didn't break his neck. He sat down to psych himself into the meeting by envisioning a successful interview with Gonzales. Whenever fears and doubts crept in, he pushed them aside. This helped to steady his nerves and resolve.

Finally, Jesse recognized a familiar rap on the door. After spying Jorge in the peephole, he opened the door. From the doorway, he saw the wiry form of a man quickly disappear around the corner.

"Was that Gonzales?"

"Nah, one of his men," said Jorge. "I need to check out the room."

Jesse let Jorge push past him into the suite. Still puzzled, he looked out the door again, feeling the same unease he'd felt in the limo. "What's he doing out there?"

Jorge walked around the room, running his hands under and around the furniture and appliances. He picked up table lamps and examined them, and even searched through the flowers and inside and outside of the vase. Then he checked behind each painting, under chairs and the bed and in between the folds of the drapes.

Stopping in front of the television set to give it a go over, Jorge finally answered Jesse, "You ask too many damn questions. Gonzales calls him Rico. He's from some other country down south." Jorge headed to the bathroom and checked it out, calling over his shoulder, "Take my word for it, *hombre*. He's bad news." When he finished, Jorge took a walkie-talkie out of his suit pocket, pushed a button and announced, "*Está bien.* It's clear."

A minute later, the door opened, revealing a thin, unassuming Mexican man in a perfectly tailored, jet black suit. Gonzales? Jesse stifled his surprise as he eyed the man, who could pass for an accountant.

"*Señor* McMillan. We meet at last, Roberto Gonzales. I'm sorry I couldn't have this chat sooner. But all good things in time, yes?" He extended a well-manicured hand to shake Jesse's, and when they finished took out a neatly folded, white handkerchief to wipe his hands.

"Very nice to meet you, *Señor* Gonzales. Shall we sit down?" Jesse motioned to the seating area. "Something to drink?"

"I never drink when I'm doing business. It's a secret I learned a long time ago," Gonzales replied as he sat down and filled the couch with his presence, despite his small stature.

"Good practice. What other survival tactics can you tell me?" Jesse said as he lowered himself into an armchair and grabbed his notepad and pen from the coffee table.

Gonzales let out a surprisingly deep laugh and flashed a disarming smile. "Already asking about my secrets! You are a reporter, and a fine one."

"Thanks," Jesse said, trying to assess the man, noting the smooth, charming way about him.

"How can I help you, *Señor* McMillan?"

"The newspaper assigned me to do an investigative piece on the plight of inner-city Santa Ana youth and drug addiction—particularly to crack cocaine."

Gonzales shook his head. "A most distressing fact of the streets, but I want to make it very clear that this is not something we condone or support in any way."

"Yes, Jorge made that perfectly clear, sir. I simply want your opinion on what appears to be an epidemic. Considering you also grew up on the same mean streets."

Gonzales smiled again, but Jesse noted that the corners of his mouth appeared taut. "I did spend some time on the streets of Santa Ana during some impressionable years, yes, but I was actually born in Mexico and attended private school in Mexico City."

Information Jesse failed to dig up during his research on the kingpin. "Oh, forgive me, sir, I didn't know that."

Gonzales's smile loosened. "My family moved here when I was fourteen years old. For the proverbial better life. But I prefer that to be off the record, *Señor* McMillan. I wouldn't want to offend my mother in any way; God rest her soul," he said.

Jesse nodded, noting the tinge of irony in the man's tone. He suspected the story behind the move to be an intriguing one, but Gonzales obviously didn't want any of that to come to light, so Jesse decided to stick to the task at hand and get the answers he came for.

"You may know that the DEA recently announced crack cocaine as one of the most highly addictive drugs on the streets. Do you have any comments about this, especially in regard to the fact that children as young as ten are becoming dependent on the substance?"

Gonzales shifted on the couch to look more directly at Jesse. "As the new drug on the block, so to speak, and I'm told a particularly powerful one, there's great demand out there for crack cocaine. My people tend to have the supply. It's simple business. But we never sell to children, and we never will. My organization has strict repercussions for doing so."

"Repercussions?"

"No need to go into details, but suffice it to say there are severe consequences for not abiding by this rule."

"In that case, do you have any idea who could be supplying the drugs to the children?"

Gonzales shifted in his seat. "*Claro*, I do," he said. "Though my organization is the strongest, it is not the only one."

"The others?"

"The Vietnamese organization has infiltrated parts of the southland, although they are young and tend to stick to their own neighborhoods in Garden Grove. And then there are those *perros*, the Italian Mafia. They are the ones supplying drugs to children," Gonzales spat out, his fists clenching and unclenching.

"And that offends you?"

Gonzales gave a mirthless laugh. "Offends me, yes. They also deserve retribution for the killing of *Señor* Mendez."

Jesse heard about that a few months ago. They found the man lying in a pool of blood in a parking garage. The official story was a mugging gone wrong.

"Wasn't Mendez your personal lawyer?"

Gonzales sucked his teeth and shifted in his seat, a dark veil suddenly shading his eyes. "*Estas preguntas*," he muttered.

"Questions are part of my job, *Señor*," said Jesse, pen poised on the notepad, hoping Gonzales continued.

"Maybe it is time," the mob kingpin said finally, his shoulders slackening slightly. "Jorge tells me I can trust you."

"You can, *Señor*," Jesse said, while Jorge continued to stand behind his boss looking straight ahead.

"Where I come from, *Señor* McMillan, we believe in honor and loyalty."

"I understand," said Jesse. He felt as if Gonzales might reveal something important and held still, afraid the slightest shift might change the kingpin's mind.

"I will tell you the truth. Cross me and you are dead."

"I'm here to share your insight and add credibility to the story. That's all."

"You are not doing this for me."

"You're right. I want recognition for good work. And if I can bring attention to the drug epidemic among the children and get help for some of them, that's icing on the proverbial cake." Jesse waited, swallowing the lead weight that had settled in his throat.

"I knew Hector Mendez. *Era mi hermano.*"

"Your brother? I had no idea."

"No one did. Hector chose to use my mother's maiden name. I took my father's name, so as not to confuse matters with our business dealings. Hector was my younger brother. Before she passed on, *mi mamá* made me promise to take care of him."

Jesse couldn't believe the information coming to him. "Is this on the record?" he asked.

"*Sí, Señor* McMillan."

Jesse waited, sensing that Gonzales wished to say more.

After several moments, his face contorted suddenly and he spat out, "That two-bit half-breed will pay for this. On my mother's grave, he'll pay. Print that *Señor* McMillan."

"What half-breed?"

"I've said enough that is newsworthy. *No mas.*"

Gonzales rose and buttoned his suit jacket. "Good day, *Señor* McMillan."

Jesse rose to shake his hand and thanked him, "*Gracias, Señor.*"

Without another word, Gonzales wiped his hands with his handkerchief and then left the room, Jorge following him.

Jesse sat back down, his mind whirling at what just happened. Not only did he get Gonzales on record—an unheard-of feat in itself—the kingpin had fingered the culprits selling drugs to kids and shared the bombshell about who killed his brother, a Mexican mob lawyer. Jesse hit the trifecta! The story would certainly put his name on the lips of editors and publishers.

He checked out of the hotel and headed home, anxious to hit the computer and let the words flow. Back at his condo, he slammed the door, sat down and worked Gonzales's information into the drug story he'd been writing. It took several hours to make it flow, but by midnight he'd nailed it. Wanting to get it to Burt right away, he dialed his home number.

Burt answered. "Yeah?"

"It's Jesse. Sorry it's late."

"I know you're not calling to wish me Merry Christmas."

Immersed in the story, Jesse had completely forgotten. "Oh, crap, that's right, it's Christmas Eve."

"Christmas Day now."

"I finished the kids on crack cocaine story with Gonzales's input. Can you give it a read over?"

"Fax it to my house."

Twenty minutes passed and the phone rang.

"McMillan, this is dynamite. You can corroborate this?"

"I can't guarantee that Gonzales will ever repeat this, and they didn't let me tape-record the conversations, so it's my word, but I did check with a source, and he and Hector Mendez were brothers."

"Okay, we'll go with that. You got a bulletproof vest?"

"No."

"Get one. I'm printing this tonight."

7

Jesse hung up the phone with Burt and felt the tension that had hounded him for weeks slip from his body. He'd done it—talked to Gonzales and survived. And perhaps even more amazing, he had pleased Burt. Never in Jesse's five years working for the man had he heard him say a story was damn good. Pretty good or passable, maybe. But never damn good.

Though exhaustion had burrowed into his bones, Jesse's excitement at seeing the story in print kept him awake. He also wanted to be available in case Burt called with any last-minute questions. So, he sat down to watch television and wait for the paper to hit the pavement outside of his condo. As if sensing the importance of the occasion, Millicent hopped into Jesse's lap to demand a good rub down—afterward curling up into a ball and snoozing.

Finally, after braving an old-time cowboy and Indian movie and exercise infomercials, around five in the morning, Jesse heard the paper deliveryman brake his truck in front of the condo, and seconds later the paper slapped the sidewalk. After removing a grouchy cat from his lap, Jesse went outside to snag the *Times*, pulling it from a plastic sleeve to see the front page as he came back inside. His was the top story:

MEXICAN MAFIA CHIEF WANTS REVENGE

Hector Mendez, brother of Roberto Gonzales, killed by rival gang. Drug king vows "los perros" will pay for the murder and accuses them of selling crack cocaine to children.

Jesse stood in the middle of his living room and read the story. Burt printed the piece almost word for word, which gave him a surge of pride. When he finished reading, he mollified Millicent with an early breakfast and made himself a cup of strong coffee.

At seven o'clock, he called his parents' house and got his mother on the phone.

"Merry Christmas, Mom," he said when she answered.

"And what a Christmas. Your father's hogging the paper," she said. "I'm just about ready to go buy my own copy. I'm worried about you, honey. Talking to drug dealers?"

"I'm an investigative reporter," said Jesse. "We don't do dog-napping stories."

"I know, but *drug dealers?*"

"I just wanted to make sure you saw the article and to let you know that I'll be over in a couple of hours, if that's okay."

"It's more than okay. I'm glad you don't have one of your deadlines. I just put the turkey in the oven."

Jesse hung up the phone and marveled at his mother's naiveté when it came to drugs. Even when they lived in the Zone, knee-deep in Panama Red, when she heard the term snow in the middle of the tropics, she honestly thought people were talking about the stuff that falls from the sky.

Though he hadn't done cocaine in years—since Panama—Jesse vividly remembered the rush of heart-thumping adrenaline.

Randy talked Jesse and Lorraine into trying coke one night as they sat bored at the yacht club.

"C'mon guys. It's the best high you'll ever experience."

"That again," said Lorraine. "What's with this coke thing? Did Sam get you stuck on this?"

"No, he doesn't really do it much, but I've done it a few times. I just think you guys will like it."

A Panamanian-Italian who stood 6'2" and bench pressed 300 pounds, Sam Elvia made most Zonians and Panamanians who hung out in the Zone uneasy. They knew that his father drank and beat him, until Sam overpowered him one night. Known for the plastic trash bags full of pot that he bought in the Panamanian countryside and sold for twenty-five dollars each, Sam liked to throw them over his shoulder and shout, "Ho, ho, ho. What do you prefer? Naughty or nice?"

The girls found it funny; the guys counted out their cash. Not many people talked to Sam, except Randy, who had no fear of him, but instead looked up to him with unabashed awe.

On that particular night, Jesse and Lorraine gave in to Randy's urging and agreed to try cocaine. They all piled into Sam's '73 Camaro and traveled to a beat-up apartment building in downtown Panama.

"Sam, my man, who's the groupies?" said the bony guy with glassy eyes, who answered the door.

"They're cool. Everybody, this is Larn. He's from the Atlantic side," said Sam. Jesse knew a few people from that side of the Zone, which had a significantly smaller population than the Pacific side where Jesse lived and an even more laid-back lifestyle that included a lot of time spent on the beach.

Larn flipped his long, dirty-blond hair back with a quick shake of his head, eyed Lorraine and strode to the other side of the room. At an old wooden chest, he pulled a clear plastic bag out of the top drawer and held it up for everyone to see. "This is that primo stuff I been passing your way, Sammy."

"Great," said Sam. "Break it out. We've got a couple virgins."

"No shit, I didn't think there were any virgins left in the Zone."

Larn took a small spoon from the top of the chest and sat down at a card table in the center of the room, motioning for everyone to sit in the folding chairs around it.

He spooned a small lump of powder onto a hand mirror and separated the pile into three thin lines with the edge of a razor blade. Then he handed Randy a tightly rolled up dollar bill. Balancing the mirror on one hand, Randy put the money to his nose like a straw and quickly sniffed up one line of coke. He wiped the tip of his index finger on the mirror where the line had been, picking up the leftover dust, and ran his finger over his gums. Jesse took the mirror next and hesitated.

"Go on, Jess, you'll love it," said Randy. All eyes on Jesse, he lifted the bill to his nose and snorted the coke deep into his nostril.

Once Jesse finished, Larn took the mirror and held it out to Lorraine. "What about you, pretty *chica?*"

"Maybe pretty *chica* doesn't want any," Jesse said, feeling a surge of irritation.

"Yes, I do," said Lorraine, her blue eyes defiant as she held her long blonde hair back with one hand and snorted up the line with the other.

Not until they left Larn's apartment a few minutes later did Jesse notice his heart beating extra fast, as if it actually moved in his chest. And he suddenly started talking—about anything and everything—with Randy yammering right along with him.

"Let's go back to the yacht club and show them suckers how to party. I bet the T-Birds are playing by now," said Randy.

"Whatever you want, little buddy," said Sam, who headed to the yacht club after everyone piled into his car.

"Man, I wish I was in philosophy class right now. I'd totally ace any test Mr. Miller would throw at me," said Randy, making a swipe at his nose. "I could probably even teach the class."

"Aren't you failing?" asked Lorraine, who began rifling through her purse. "I wish I had some gum. That stuff made my mouth dry."

"I've got a D. That's not failing. It don't matter anyway, cuz I'm not going to college," said Randy, who sat up front and grabbed a cigarette pack from Sam's breast pocket, extracting one for himself and lighting it.

"With that grammar, they'd kick you out of high school anyway," said Lorraine.

"You mean college?" said Randy.

"Yeah, whatever," she said, fanning the air in front of her face. "Do you have to smoke right now, Randy? It makes my hair smell horrible."

"Oh, shit, that's right. You might see dickhead at the yacht club!" Randy said.

"His name is Ricardo. I'm supposed to get a meeting with his mom about modeling really soon."

"You still buying that bull, Lorri?" asked Randy. "He wants one thing and one thing only and—"

Jesse cut him off. "So, if you had a chance to be anyone famous, who would it be?"

Randy turned around and blew smoke at him and Lorraine. "Who you asking?"

"Everyone," said Jesse.

"Well, that's easy. I want to be Batman. Or maybe Superman. Which one's faster?" Randy turned to his open car window and started to hang out of it with his arms extended, but Sam reached over and grabbed his shirt, pulling him back onto the seat.

"You're incredible, Randy," Lorraine exclaimed. "You've got the chance to be anyone you want, and you choose a cartoon character?"

"What's wrong with that? Might as well be superhuman while you're at it! What about you, Lorri? I know! What's that supermodel's name?"

"Cindy Crawford, Randy. I've told you a million, quadrillion times."

"Yeah, well, I bet she'd tell you not to frown. It makes wrinkles."

"What about you, Jesse?" asked Lorraine.

"A famous writer, of course. Like Faulkner or Steinbeck."

"That is going to be so cool one day when you're a famous writer," said Randy. "Just remember us little guys."

"And girls," said Lorraine, crossing her arms and looking out of the window as they left Panama City and headed into the Zone. Her cue she'd had enough of Randy.

"What about you, Sam? Who would you want to be?" Randy asked.

Sam nodded at the guard who waved them onto Fort Amador. "I don't know. Never thought about it. I think I'm okay as is."

When they got to the downstairs bar at the yacht club, they found

Ron, the lead singer, belting out a song and playing the harmonica in between lines of verse while a crowd cheered him on. Everyone knew Ron and his band as die-hard Zonians, who had no intention of ever leaving the laidback lifestyle of the Zone with its unending summertime vacation vibe. In his cocaine high, as Jesse watched Ron acknowledge the bass player for his playing and the resulting clapping from the crowd, Jesse experienced an epiphany. The charm of the Zone was that it was essentially like living in Neverland—that lighthearted place suspended in childhood without the responsibilities of adulthood. He and his friends and even the adults had little to worry about here in the Zone. They lived in great homes, went to good schools and had access to plenty of food available from the States at the commissary. Everyone he knew had a maid. So easy was Zone living that when Zonians tried the "real world" in the States, many came back—like Ron, who lasted a month in Florida at twenty-two, fourteen years before, and hadn't ventured out of the Zone since. Jesse worried about Ron and himself and all Zonians if Carter signed the treaties and the Canal Zone disappeared.

The next day, Jesse felt a drug letdown. The high felt ultra-high, but the low way too low. It took him several days to get over the down feelings, during which time he decided his first time was his last. So a few weeks later when Randy brought up dealing pot, Jesse was surprised and upset.

"Isn't that dangerous, Randy? I'm really worried about you."

"It's cool. Sam's got this connection in Panama City. They're looking for dealers in the Zone. Don't look so freaked out." Randy put an arm around Jesse. "I'll be fine. It's just pot—not the hard stuff."

"But your Spanish sucks. What if something goes wrong with a deal in Panama and you can't talk your way out of it?" Jesse remained unconvinced.

"Sam's teaching me enough Spanish to get by. Besides, when you say Panama Red, everyone's speaking the same language."

Jesse showed up at his parents' house, presents in hand.

"Sorry, I didn't have time to wrap them," he apologized as his mom took the gifts and put them under the tree.

"So nice of you to bring something for us, dear, but honestly, I'm just so excited to see you, and I know your father feels the same way," she said as she turned and outstretched her arms. He walked into her embrace for her signature extra-long hug that always felt as if she'd squeeze the life out of him.

"You're always so busy. I miss seeing you, sweetheart," she said, letting go of him and laying her hands softly on both of his cheeks.

Jesse smiled into her familiar gray-blue eyes and noticed how her height seemed to diminish a little each time he saw her. She'd pulled her graying hair back into a ponytail and wore over slacks and a blouse a holiday apron he'd gotten her a few years ago that said, "Merry Kissmas."

Jesse recalled the street kids he'd talked to for the article, many of whom didn't have parents who cared. "Actually, Mom, I miss your hugs. You can squeeze as hard and as long as you want."

Her face lit up with a beaming smile and she replied, "You know I have a long memory, son, I'm holding you to that!"

Jesse laughed. "Good one!"

Then she noticed the cast on his hand.

"What on earth happened?"

"Stupid accident on my bike. It's nothing."

"I've warned you about bicycling around cars here. There's so much traffic."

"It's no big deal, Mom, and I wasn't in traffic. I was on the bike trail. I'll be fine. Where's Dad?"

"He's in the den, and I've got to get back into the kitchen. I still have stuffing to make. And I've got some ceviche for appetizers to check on."

"Panama-style ceviche?"

"Of course. Is there any other kind?"

Jesse went into the back of the house and found his father in the den watching television.

"Son, good to see you," he said, attempting to stand up.

Jesse motioned him to stay seated. "It's okay, Pop, Mom told me your back's been bothering you again. No need. I'm sitting anyway." He eased into his mom's flowered armchair next to his father's and saw the newspaper with his article on the coffee table.

"Quite a story you wrote there," his father said, indicating his head toward the paper. "Proud of you."

"Thanks. How's work?" Jesse asked.

"Good. I've been thinking about retiring in the next two to three years. But enough talk about me." His father cleared his throat. "I know your mom won't ask you, but she's going to ask me, so I'll get it over with and ask for her. Any young ladies in your life?"

Jesse smiled and thought of Clare, who he tried to call before coming over but there'd been no answer. He figured she must be at her family's house.

"*Chuleta!*" His father cried. "There is someone. Your mom said she had a feeling. I guess she was right."

Jesse felt a flush warm his face. "Her name is Clare, and we originally met in Panama. I don't think you'd remember her. She came the year before we moved—an Army brat."

"What's the last name?" said Jesse's father, who worked for the Panama Canal Company when they lived there.

"Stinson."

"Name sounds familiar. How did you hook up again?"

Jesse told him how they'd met and been spending some time together, including their trip to the emergency room for his hand.

"She sounds like she doesn't scare easily," his father said when Jesse finished. "Your fingers healing okay? I'm surprised your mom didn't have a fit when she saw the cast."

"Yeah, they're going to be fine. I didn't want to worry her, so I told her I fell on my bike."

Jesse's dad nodded and said nothing more about it. Instead, they reminisced about Christmas times past, especially in Panama, including how hard they worked to get a decent pine tree in the tropics, and how some years they'd resorted to using palm trees. Jesse recalled Christmas caroling with their church, and how strange it felt to be singing about snow and hot cider in 85-degree weather.

When Jesse's mom called them in for the meal, he helped her find room on the table for the platter he'd given her that she'd piled high with turkey and stuffing. They started with crackers and Zonian ceviche, which took them all back to Panama and initiated more memories of tropical Christmases. Before Jesse left that evening, he and his father started up a batch of beer, and he promised to come back in a couple of weeks to sample it.

When Jesse got home that night, he tried calling Clare again, but still no answer. He watched a little television with Millicent in his lap and decided to call it an early night.

On the way to the paper the next day, Jesse tried to gauge the reactions of his fellow reporters regarding the article. Most likely, Becky would see the big picture and realize that the story would be good for the entire newsroom, but he wasn't sure how Phil would react.

When he got to the office, Jesse soon found out when Phil said, "Great story. Becky and I thought maybe we could all three go out for lunch. We want to ply you with a few questions about how you got your source to spill his guts like that."

Flattered, Jesse agreed to lunch, where he answered questions about his interviews with Jorge and Gonzales.

"How did you get Gonzales to open up? I can't even get the local jerk councilmen to give me anything but their home numbers," Becky exclaimed as she speared a forkful of salad.

"That and when their wives will be out of town is all the info you need," said Phil.

"Very funny," said Becky and scowled.

"I tried not to say much," offered Jesse. "I let him do all of the talking."

"Now we know Becky's problem," said Phil, breaking into a fit of laughter.

"You're hilarious, Phil," said Becky, shaking her head.

. . .

When they got back to the office, Jesse felt too distracted to work, so he organized some papers and decided to call it a day. He really wanted to see Clare, so he signed out of his computer, left the paper and headed to the botanical preserve in hopes that she'd be there.

Clare's car was the only one in the parking lot. To enter the preserve, he checked around, then pushed open an iron gate and walked under a massive violet-red flowered bougainvillea archway. Right away, he loved the feeling inside amongst all of the plants. It filled him with the same calm, quiet awe that he used to feel in the jungle. He heard the sound of water somewhere, and his senses hit overdrive at the sweet smell of jasmine and the musky odor of coastal sagebrush. Eventually, Jesse came around a retaining wall dripping with bright yellow flowers and stopped short at the sight of Clare dressed in faded jeans and a blue tank top, leaning over a bin. As she examined something in the bin, several strands of hair loosened from the big barrette at the back of her head blew across her face and she brushed them away with the back of her hand.

Jesse watched and thought how he liked that about her—how she became immersed in things she loved.

As if Clare sensed him, she looked up, surprise on her face. "Jesse! What are you doing here?"

"What's got your rapt attention?"

"Compost. Look at it." Clare scooped up a small mound of chocolate brown earth from the bin and held out her hand. "It's so rich. I can't believe how incredible it is."

"Hmmm." He studied the dirt in her hand.

"We made this in record time—just two weeks." At Jesse's blank look, she laughed and explained. "Two weeks ago this compost was horse manure, grass clippings, ground-up bark and leaves and kitchen scraps."

"What do you do with it?"

"We plant, fertilize, mulch with it. It helps plants grow."

"Where is everyone?"

"Off for Christmas today. I wanted to check on the compost, and I love it here when it's quiet."

"It's a great place," Jesse said, smiling at Clare. "Why don't you work here full time?"

"No money in it. And in all honesty, it's not enough. This place is a great testing ground, but I like working in the real world doing toxic clean ups. It's really satisfying to use technology to reverse the effects of chemical and oil spills and help the earth, and a lot more challenging."

"I guess that's the way I could look at leaving Panama," Jesse said, surprising himself with the revelation. "I sure wasn't stretching myself there, and probably never would. I can't see myself as a construction worker or in the military. Although I could have worked on a deforestation crew further south." Jesse grinned at his joke, but Clare frowned.

"Merry Christmas," Jesse said. "Did you have a good one?"

"Yes, I went to my aunt's in San Diego. My parents decided not to visit from Texas this year. It was a lot of fun. My cousin brought her baby. He's only eight months old and so adorable. You?"

"I went to my parents' in Sherman Oaks. A good day for me, too." He stopped talking for a moment and then changed the subject. "I got the interview with Gonzales on Christmas Eve. The story ran in yesterday's paper. Burt loved it. I haven't heard from Jorge, so I'm assuming Gonzales is okay with it."

Clare smiled. "That's great. I'm thrilled for—"

Jesse moved closer and brushed his thumb across her lips. "You're taking my breath away with the light shining in your hair," he told her, leaning in to kiss her, his heart thumping at the softness of her lips beneath his.

She pulled away. "Jesse, you've got to be kidding. I'm such a mess."

"You're perfect," he said, pressing against her and kissing her neck, which smelled faintly of roses.

Clare laughed slightly and sighed. "Go on, I love it when you talk sweet to me."

"Let's see what more sweet nothings I can come up with," said Jesse, trailing kisses along the side of her neck, which caused a sharp intake in her breath. "Roses are red, violets are...Are they really blue?" he asked, this time pulling her even closer as he explored the other side of her neck. Clare laced her fingers around the back of his neck and ran the tip of her tongue across his lips. This sent a lightning bolt of desire through Jesse that inspired him to guide her to the shade of a nearby tree, the grass beneath green and soft.

Jesse didn't care that they had no blanket to spread out or even about his casted hand. All he knew was that he wanted Clare. When he took hold of the hem of her shirt with his good hand, she held her arms up as he pulled it over her head and dropped it to the ground. Then she guided his shirt over his head and peppered his chest with kisses before unzipping his pants and sliding out of her jeans and panties.

When Clare finished undressing by unclasping her bra, the sight of her nude body in front of him sent Jesse's body ablaze. He eased himself down onto the grass, looking up at her, while in one fluid movement she lowered herself, straddling him. Pulling the barrette from her hair, she let her mane cascade down her back and over her shoulders and then held his gaze as she guided him into her. The moment they joined, she moaned and rocked her hips slowly. Above him with her bare breasts and long, silken hair, she looked like a goddess—his goddess, come to claim him. Jesse had made love with plenty of women, but the way Clare stroked his chest, nibbled his lips and his neck and murmured his name felt like nothing he'd ever experienced. He held back, letting her decide as she moved in sync with him, knowing and waiting for just the right time until every synapse in his brain seemed to explode. When they finished loving one another and she leaned forward, her face inches from his, he saw a tear slip down her face. Licking it off her cheek, he murmured, "That was incredible."

Clare slid off Jesse to sit cross-legged beside him as he stretched out on the damp ground. Making love to her surpassed what he remembered from that first time in her parent's trailer in Panama. She was no longer a shy girl, but a woman sure of herself. Her skin looked so flawless and lovely in the sunlight; he wanted to devour every inch of her again.

"I've thought about this for a very long time," Jesse said.

Clare gazed at him with questions in her eyes. "I didn't expect—"

"Me to attack you here? I didn't either, but I'm glad I did."

Clare said nothing.

"Is it Bob?"

"That's part of it. It's— Did you do this because you're excited about the story turning out so well?"

Baffled by Clare's question, Jesse asked, "What do you mean?"

"I know men get turned on when they're successful. Act on instincts."

"I won't argue with instincts here, but it has nothing to do with the story. I've wanted you since the day I met you on the Causeway, and I think we can have a really good thing." Jesse waited, thinking how he would plead with her, if that's what it took. Every inch of him hoped she would agree they were meant to be together.

Clare sat silent for a moment and then took Jesse's right hand in hers and opened it up, kissing the palm. When she finished, she said, "Yes, violets really are blue."

That reminded Jesse of the bracelet. "I got something for you." He reached for his pants and removed the small box.

Clare's eyes lit up with surprise as she took the gift. "A Christmas present!"

"Open it."

She lifted the lid off the box and took out the bracelet, laughing when she saw the tiny flowers woven into the chain. "Violets!"

"And they're blue," said Jesse, taking the bracelet, unclasping it and securing it on her wrist. "What do you say? Are you willing to give us a try? I hope you don't say no."

Clare ran a fingertip over the bracelet. And then so softly that he could barely hear her, she replied, "Okay, Jesse McMillan. Let's do this."

8

The next morning, Jesse watched as Clare slept beside him. They had come home the night before with pizza, hopped into bed to eat it and ended up talking until three in the morning. Jesse knew Clare was a military brat, but didn't realize that meant living in eight places before she turned eighteen. She especially liked living on an island off the coast of Washington state accessible only by a small boat. There she made her first best friend, only to lose her to a drunk driving accident when the two were thirteen.

Jesse shared that adjusting to California weather after a lifetime in the tropics challenged him. He told Clare how he hated the feel of the chilly Pacific Ocean the first time it touched his toes and how overwhelmed he initially became when driving the freeway, which felt like navigating the arms of an octopus. At one point, he found himself sharing with Clare what it felt like growing up in the Zone and being an American, but not ever really feeling like one.

"Being a Zonian meant having an allegiance to the Zone and the way of life there," Jesse tried to explain. "In many ways, we lived in an altered universe—but our universe. We had our own code of ethics and standards of living—basically live and let live, providing you always stood up for the Zone."

"What about Southern California?" Clare asked at one point. "You've lived here for nearly a decade."

Jesse thought for a minute and replied, "I love my job. But, since leaving Panama, it's like I've been living in a temporary holding pattern, circling over the airport, but never landing."

"It must have been hard leaving your childhood home so abruptly," Clare said.

The straightforward way she made the statement stopped Jesse short, and he suddenly felt a despair he hadn't experienced in a long time.

"Leaving Panama was the hardest thing I've ever done," Jesse admitted. "The morning we got on the plane to leave, it sounds crazy, but I nearly threw up. I still get nauseated when I smell diesel like you do at the airport. I feel for people like the Vietnamese refugees who've had to escape their own countries. Not exactly like that for me, because I can go back if I want to, but the truth is there's nothing to go back to. Everything changed once the Panamanians took ownership. They understandably wanted to reclaim the Zone as their own, and they did make the land just another piece of Panama. Unfortunately, that meant letting things fall into disrepair. I'm told there are buildings sitting empty that are nearly unrecognizable."

When he finished talking, Clare stroked his cheek and kissed him on the forehead.

"Sorry, I must sound infantile to you with all of your moves as a kid," said Jesse.

"Losing a way of life is hard, because in some ways it means letting go of those relationships that meant so much to you. Without that context of place and time, people drift apart, and even with the people you do stay in contact with, the relationships are never really the same. That doesn't mean, though, that you can't redefine relationships in a good way," Clare said, snuggling up so close to Jesse that he felt her heart beating against his as they both drifted off to sleep.

Now as he watched her sleeping next to him, Jesse marveled at Clare's insight. She had a way of seeing the truths that many people just never would, and she grounded him in a way no one ever had.

When she woke a few minutes later and arched her body in a languorous stretch, she said, "Orange juice."

"That's what you think the minute your eyes are open?"

"Some people need coffee in the morning. I need orange juice."

"I think I have a can in the freezer." He threw back the sheet, but Clare reached out and grabbed his arm.

"Jesse, wait."

He looked at her, hoping she wanted to make love again.

"We need to talk."

"Go ahead."

"I need to know where we stand."

"Is this about Bob?"

"Bob's not right for me. I've always known that, and it's not fair to let things continue with him. What I want to talk about is you and me. I just have to know."

"What?"

"If last night was a one-time occurrence—or should I say two-time." She gave a slight smile.

"I hope not," said Jesse. "Like I told you in the botanical garden yesterday, I really care for you."

She sighed. "I want to believe you."

"Then do," Jesse said, kissing her nose and ducking out of the room to get her orange juice.

Another typical Saturday night beach party. Jesse and his friends had parked their cars on the sand a little ways off the road. Some started a small bonfire, while others hung out at their cars with radios blaring. Jesse had invited Pablo to come along, which turned out to be a good thing, because Randy just wanted to lie on the hood of Sam's car and talk about playing the bongos for the T-Birds.

"You'll play great, little buddy," Sam said every few minutes as he swigged from a bottle of Panama beer and rocked the car for emphasis. "Go for it."

Pablo and Jesse decided to walk down to the water. When they got close, they both kicked off their sandals and padded through the powdery, white sand. Jesse welcomed the warm water that soon washed up to submerge his feet. The two walked in silence for a time, the only sound the faint hiss of the seawater pulling away from the sand.

"I can almost hear you thinking, my friend," said Pablo finally. "It is about the treaties, no?"

Jesse sighed. "Yes, it looks like Carter is going to sign, isn't he? And we'll be saying goodbye to the Zone."

"From what I have heard from my uncle and father, yes, you are correct. Carter is likely to sign."

Jesse stopped in his tracks at the water's edge and looked up at the sky, as if searching for reassurance amidst the thousands of shimmering stars.

"Ah, the brilliant *estrellas de* Panama, they are like no other," said Pablo, who also looked up.

"Panama is like no other," said Jesse, inhaling the moist, briny breeze.

"What will you do when the treaties are signed?" asked Pablo.

"That's something I haven't thought about at all," admitted Jesse. "I can barely wrap my head around losing the Zone."

Just then Jesse thought he heard a shriek. "Did you hear something?"

"What?" asked Pablo.

"It sounded like someone crying out."

"Probably a lovers' quarrel."

"Oh, my God, please don't!" a girl screamed up ahead.

Jesse filled with cold horror. "That's Lorraine!"

"Look, *puta*, I have lost patience with you!"

They broke into a run toward the sound of their voices.

Jesse and Pablo found them illuminated by the night sky, Ricardo on top of Lorraine, her skirt hiked up around her waist. In the split second he realized someone had arrived, Ricardo jumped up and swung around. While Jesse ran to Lorraine's side, Pablo lunged at Ricardo, and the two landed in the sand.

"*Pendejo!*" Pablo yelled, his fist hitting Ricardo's jaw.

"You are an asshole!" Ricardo shouted as he tried to push Pablo off. "You love gringos more than your own people!"

At that comment, Pablo froze, clenched his fists and got up off Ricardo. "Get out of here before I kill you."

Ricardo sprang up, gave them all a dirty look and ran off into the night.

"Are you okay, Lorri?" Jesse asked, once he'd gone.

Lorraine's face crumpled and she buried it in Jesse's shoulder. "I'm so embarrassed and stupid. You warned me."

"Don't blame yourself. He's an asshole, and he led you on with that modeling mumbo jumbo."

Lorraine pulled free from Jesse's grasp and stood up, trying to smooth her clothes and hair. "I don't want anyone to know about this. Let's just go back to the car."

As they headed to the party, Jesse thought about what might have happened if he and Pablo hadn't come along. The thought made him livid and relieved at the same time.

Jesse led Lorraine to Randy's car, where they leaned side-by-side against the hood. Despite the warm night, Lorraine shivered, so Jesse hugged her to him. At that moment, Clare and Missy approached, and he and Clare looked directly at one another. Averting her eyes, Clare whispered in Missy's ear and the two turned around and headed back from where they came. Jesse thought about going after her, but realized he'd have nothing to say that would make any sense.

Not until later that night after Jesse and Randy delivered Lorraine safely home did the enormity of what happened hit him. Suddenly, anger consumed Jesse, firing up a desire for revenge.

"What's up, man? asked Randy. "You haven't said a word since the beach party tonight. You all right?"

Jesse proceeded to do what he promised he wouldn't do and told Randy everything.

"That pervert!" yelled Randy. "Ricardo has to pay."

Jesse didn't have the energy to argue with Randy, and truthfully, he hoped that Ricardo paid dearly.

They didn't see Ricardo at school for two weeks, and when he did come, he arrived in a wheelchair. The official story was that he broke both legs skiing in the States, but Jesse found out later that Randy had told Sam what happened to Lorraine.

After holding and reassuring Clare before her goodbye meeting with Bob, Jesse left his condo and headed for the *Times*. Burt was waiting by his desk when he got in.

"Vacation's over McMillan, time to get cracking. I want an entire Panama series. That place is full of good copy, and I know you can get me plenty of inside dirt."

"I thought we're getting a lot of good stuff from the wire?"

"Why would I rely on wire copy when I have you? Put some fresh angles on my desk by the end of the day," demanded Burt. "And I want some juicy Panamanian characters in the story. Someone like Gonzales—not that goofball Noriega. Someone everyone admires and looks up to—like Omar Torrijos. As I recall, they loved him, and a lot of people were really upset when his plane went down."

Jesse nodded, thinking of Pablo's devastation when his favorite uncle died.

"Look, McMillan. The Gonzales story is old news," said Burt. "My nose tells me you know a lot more about Panama than you're saying—so out with it."

9

Delivered by the mail clerk, the message arrived just as Jesse prepared to leave the office for the day. It came in a small, white envelope with his name in loopy script.

"Hey, where'd this come from?" he called after the mail clerk.

"Some guy dropped it off at the front desk a little while ago. That's all the receptionist told me."

Standing next to his desk, Jesse tore open the envelope and pulled out a piece of white notepaper that read:

Gringo: The Gonzales story was skillfully written, but I'm surprised and disappointed. You're usually more thorough. Perhaps you're rattled about what's going on in your former home?

Jesse sank into his chair and double-checked the paper and envelope for any information that could tell him where the note came from, but nothing. Who the hell wrote this? And why an unnamed pen pal mentioning Panama? It read like a male, and possibly Latino, since he called him gringo. Jesse sat there for a few minutes scanning his memory bank, but came up blank. Was there more to the Mendez murder? And what did Panama have to do with it? Jesse had heard other investigative reporters talk about nut jobs contacting them after they wrote a big story, so that could be happening here. Now that he thought about it, though,

Jesse had to admit that the Mendez story had been very pat. That worried him on many levels. For one, he didn't want anything coming back to bite him on the ass at the paper. For another, it made him uneasy to know that someone watched him so closely. He'd obviously known Jesse was in the office.

Glancing at his watch, he noted the time. Six o'clock. He'd promised to meet Clare at his condo at seven—for dinner, cooked by him now that his hand felt a little better—so he needed to go grocery shopping.

A little more than an hour later, he pulled into his carport and saw Clare sitting on his front porch. He regretted making her wait and thought, maybe I should give her a key. The image of Clare putting her clothes in one of his drawers made him smile as he walked up the sidewalk toward her, swinging the grocery bag.

"Waiting long?"

"About fifteen minutes. But it's okay. I was early. Here," she said, holding out another white envelope. "Someone dropped this off for you."

The smile on Jesse's face turned to a frown as he grabbed the envelope from her and scanned the complex.

"What's the matter?"

"Let's get inside." Jesse handed Clare his keys so she could open the door. Once they stood in his entryway, he set the grocery bag on the floor and shut and bolted the door.

"You're alarming me, Jesse," said Clare. "What's going on?"

He held up a finger and ripped open the envelope to see the familiar writing.

Hi again, Gringo. It's not surprising you live in Irvine. It's a lot like the Zone. Speaking of your former home, expect a visitor very soon.

Clare reached for the letter, and Jesse gave it to her.

"Who is this from?" she asked after reading it.

"Your guess is as good as mine," he said and shrugged, pulling the other letter out of his pants pocket. "I got this one before I left the paper."

She read that note and said, "Obviously, this person knows you lived in the Canal Zone. Seems fixated by it."

"The handwriting in both notes looks the same."

Clare nodded. "Looks like a man's writing."

"That's what I'm thinking. What I can't figure out is who the hell it is. What did the guy who brought the note look like?"

"It was a kid. He came right before you got here. He was looking for you, so I took the envelope."

"Okay, wish I'd been here to ask who paid him to deliver it."

"Sorry, I would've asked, if I'd known."

"It's not your fault. I should apologize for getting you into this mess. This is probably not what you signed up for."

"What is this, exactly?"

"I wish I could tell you."

A rapping on the door jolted them both, but Jesse relaxed when he heard his neighbor Tony's voice. He unbolted the door and swung it open.

"Hey, man, long time since we hung out, so I came to see if you wanted to pop a brew and watch a game, but I see you have company," said Tony.

"It's okay, come in." Jesse motioned him inside and shut the door.

"Okay, I'm intrigued," said Tony, who saw Jesse's casted hand. "What's up? And what's with the cast?"

"Occupational health hazard."

Tony's eyebrows flew up. "You on a heavy story?"

"It's looking that way."

"Listen, you need any backup, just let me know," said Tony. "No questions asked. I'm thinking about applying to the police academy, so I'm pumped to get a little practice."

"Thanks for the offer. I may take you up on it."

Jesse saw Clare checking Tony out. Most girls did. He worked construction, and his mounded biceps and thick, muscular thighs announced that fact.

"I like your new security guard," said Tony, returning the favor and eyeing Clare.

She chuckled, and said, "I gave up trying to save Jesse a long time ago."

"We know each other from my Panama days," explained Jesse, handing Tony the letters. "What do you think of these? A kid delivered the bottom one a few minutes ago."

Tony read the notes and then whistled. "Sounds like a real creeper, man. Weird how he talks about the Canal Zone. You think this has anything to do with that Mendez character you wrote about recently?"

"I think we could bet on it," said Jesse, taking the notes and setting them on his dining room table while Clare picked up the grocery bag from the floor and headed for the kitchen.

"Like I said, I'm here if you need me," said Tony, turning to leave. "Have a good night."

"You can stay if you want," offered Clare. "It looks like Jesse got enough steak to feed an army."

At the mention of steak, Tony perked up. "You sure? I'll help you grill, and I'll clear out after we eat. How's that?"

Jesse nodded, thinking that the delivered messages had squashed any chance of romance, anyway.

Later that night after Clare planted up containers of vegetable plants for his patio and then left, Jesse wondered about the mysterious author. On impulse, he called Jorge.

"McMillan, I thought I finally got rid of your ass."

"Something came up," said Jesse.

"Something always does, and it ain't putting any *dinero* in my pocket."

"I'm getting written messages from someone."

"Notes? I can't help you with love letters, *amigo*."

"The notes mention the article."

"What kind of bullshit do they say?"

"They suggest the story wasn't thorough, and they keep mentioning Panama."

"There's always more to every story," said Jorge.

"And what about Panama?"

"What about it? Look, McMillan, I gotta go."

Jesse put down the receiver, thinking how Jorge hung up awfully fast. He decided to flip on the tube for news on the Noriega manhunt. After channel surfing for a minute, he found a foreign correspondent reporting that the military leader continued to elude capture. Watching the burning cars and looting in the background, Jesse prayed they'd get Noriega soon so the madness could stop.

Beat from the long day, Jesse stayed in his recliner and watched a few sitcoms, eventually drifting off to sleep. When something woke him a few hours later, he sat up and switched off the TV, which had transformed to fuzz. A sharp knocking on the door made him jump up. Who the hell could be here at this hour? It was probably three in the morning. Then he remembered that Micky sometimes came over to crash after drinking too much at the local bar.

Jesse looked through the front door peephole at the back of a head of jet black, curly hair. Definitely not Micky. His heart thudded at the thought of this being the mysterious scribbler.

"Who is it?" he called out.

"A friend," said the visitor, turning around.

Jesse recognized the voice immediately. Yanking the door open, he came face-to-face with his old friend Pablo.

10

Pablo stood on the porch, a worn and dirty piece of paper clutched in his hand. Jesse hardly recognized his old friend. Unlike the good-looking guy he'd known in Panama, Pablo's clothes were disheveled, eyes bloodshot, and his once close-cropped hair an unruly mop.

"Jesse, I'm glad I found you."

"Pablo, what the hell happened to you?" said Jesse, pulling him across the threshold and shutting the door.

"It's been a long time, *amigo*," said Pablo, hugging Jesse to him and pounding him on the back.

"Nearly a decade," confirmed Jesse. "Sorry, this isn't all that fancy, but come on in."

Pablo looked around Jesse's condo and his face crumpled. "Everything's gone. I have nowhere to go."

"Everything? What do you mean?"

Pablo sank to the edge of the couch and put his head in his hands. "They killed *mi papá*."

"Oh, my God. Who did?"

"Noriega's men. Last week. They're keeping it quiet."

Jesse felt afraid to ask. "What about your mother and sister?"

"In Peru. My father and I packed them up a few weeks ago and sent them away."

"I'm sorry Pablo. I don't know what to say."

"I have not told *mi mamá*. It was hard enough for her to leave her home," said Pablo. "This will break her heart. She begged Papá and me to go with her." He sat in silence while Jesse struggled to find words to ease his old friend's pain. He noticed how incredibly thin Pablo looked.

"Are you hungry? I've got some steak in the fridge."

"*Sí, gracias*, I can't remember when I last ate."

While Jesse heated the steak on the stove, he stole a quick glance at Pablo, who sat in stony silence.

"This is a little hot," Jesse said when he set the steak and a knife and fork on the coffee table. "Can I get you anything else? Some bread?"

Pablo shook his head. "This is more than enough. Thank you."

Jesse sat back down in his recliner and watched Pablo eat.

"You must be wondering what happened," Pablo finally said, wiping his mouth clean.

"Do you need to lay low? Just tell me."

Pablo sighed and stared straight ahead as he spoke.

"For months there has been unrest in Panama—long before they tried to arrest Noriega. A subversive faction of Noriega's army plotted a takeover for more than a year." Pablo paused.

"Is that who killed your father?"

"Yes. *Mi mamá* wanted us all to leave. She said that Panama no longer welcomed us, and we would be safer in Peru. But *mi papá* was a stubborn man, and he had his *orgullo*, his pride. Without that pride, he said, he would die," said Pablo, who bolted up and began pacing the room. "They gunned him down in front of our building after he returned from an anti-revolt meeting. He had been a strong force against them, and they did what they do with men they fear."

Jesse waited for his friend to continue.

"I found him soon after he was shot, and my father told me to run—to get out of Panama. I didn't want to leave him, but he said that I had to protect myself. Those were his last words to me."

Tears crept from the corners of Pablo's eyes, stealing down his lean cheeks as he sat back down on the couch. "He lay there bleeding on the sidewalk. I tried to help him stand so we could run, but he told me that *la policía* probably heard the shots and would soon come. If they caught me, they would accuse me of shooting him and throw me in prison. I would never be able to honor his wishes. So, he told me to leave him there, which I did, like a *perro*. For that I will never forgive myself."

Jesse got up and put a hand on his friend's shoulder as his body shook with silent sobs. When Pablo finished, Jesse cleared away his dish and grabbed bedding from the hall closet. He returned to the living room to find his friend lying on the couch, already half asleep. Jesse handed him a pillow for his head and covered him with a blanket.

Pablo looked up at Jesse with a half-smile. "When my father told me to leave Panama, my first thought was to come to you in the States, my good friend," said Pablo.

"I'm honored you thought of me," said Jesse. "I'll help you however I can."

In what was left of the night, Jesse slept fitfully, dreaming about Pablo's father, smiling one minute and lying in a pool of blood the next.

At six in the morning, Jesse awoke with an unsettling realization. The note had been right! An old friend from Panama had come to visit. He tried to sleep, but the unease of so obviously being watched unsettled him. He left a note with his work number on the coffee table next to a still sleeping Pablo and slipped out the front door.

When he arrived at the paper, there was no one in the newsroom but a copy editor. Jesse sat down at his desk. Who could he call in Panama to find out more about how Pablo's father died? Who could actually get through the Panamanian red tape and find out the truth? He knew the obvious answer, but couldn't possibly call her now. He hadn't talked to her in almost ten years. Not since that morning. He'd have to find another source.

Fifteen minutes later after searching his contacts and coming up with no one else, he slammed his fist on his desk. "Fuck!"

"Get laid on your own time, McMillan. What the hell you doing in here at this hour?" Burt appeared out of nowhere, a large coffee in one hand, the *Wall Street Journal* in the other.

"We have to talk, boss," said Jesse.

"Come into my office," Burt said, heading across the room. "I hope you got some good juice on Panama. Wallerstein expects a lot of you nowadays."

"If he expects so much of me, why doesn't he pay me more?" said Jesse, moving a stack of newspapers he found on a chair to the floor and sitting down.

"That's what you want to talk about, McMillan? A raise?"

"No, this is much bigger than any raise I'll ever get." Jesse told Burt about the mysterious notes and Pablo's visit.

As Jesse talked, Burt leaned forward. "You got someone you can call about the death?"

"I'm working on it. I can't call just anyone. Pablo says they're trying to deep-six this one, and I know he'd like to know more."

"Yeah, him and us. You're a smart guy. You'll figure it out. Now get outta here and get to work." Burt cracked open his newspaper, dismissing Jesse.

Back at his desk, Jesse called his mom and got the number; then picked up the phone to dial, but instead cradled the receiver. How could he call Lorraine out of the blue after all this time?

"Just pick up the phone and call her," said Randy. "You've called her a million times before. It's no big deal."

"It is a big deal," said Jesse. "All those million times before I didn't like her. Things are different now."

"You are such a damn pussy. You know Lorraine's crazy about you."

They stood next to the phone in Jesse's living room. He and Randy had double-dated the night before with Missy and Lorraine, and Randy wanted them to go out again.

"I just saw her last night. She's going to think I'm desperate or something."

"You are!"

Jesse took a swing at Randy, who laughed and jumped out of the way.

"Missy told me Lorraine's hot for you."

"She did?" Jesse felt a pleasant, warm feeling wash through him at the thought. He wiped his sweaty palms on his jeans and then dialed her number.

She picked up on the second ring. "Hello?"

"Lorraine?"

"Oh, hi Jesse."

Jesse took a deep breath and then said, "There's a party at the Diablo Spinning Club tonight, and I'm calling to see if you want to come with me, Randy and Missy."

"Sure," said Lorraine.

After he hung up, Randy said, "Let me guess. She said yes."

Jesse nodded.

"I knew she would! And don't kill me or anything, but Missy never did say that Lorraine is hot for you."

"What the hell, Randy! Why'd you lie to me?"

"Because you needed some courage. It worked, didn't it?"

Jesse picked up the newsroom phone and dialed the long distance number.

"General Wilhelm's office."

"Lorraine?"

"Yes, who's this?"

"It's me, Lorraine. It's Jesse."

Silence for a moment, and then Lorraine stammered, "Jesse, this is a surprise. It's been awhile."

"That's an understatement."

"My mom told me you're living in California. How are you doing?"

"I'm doing good, Lorraine, but how about you? I know it's been rough there."

"It's been pretty awful. You can't imagine how terrible it is to see the Zone so trashed. Things have changed a lot. You'd hardly recognize it. And Panama City is even worse."

"I hear you hooked up with a jarhead."

"His name is Kurt, and adults call them Marines."

"Sorry. I've never been much good at being an adult. I don't know if your mom told you, but I'm an investigative reporter now."

"She said something about it," said Lorraine.

"I'm working on a story about Panama, and I need some information." Jesse told her about Pablo and his father and asked if she could check into his death.

"Well, if the executive assistant to the General at the highest command level in Panama can't dig something up, no one can," she said. "Let me see what I can find out."

"That would be great. Thanks Lorraine. And it's really good to hear your voice."

"Good to talk to you, too, Jesse, but don't thank me yet."

When the phone rang a couple of hours later, Jesse was surprised to hear Lorraine's voice again.

"Jesse, I've got some really interesting information for you."

"Tell me."

"Pablo's father was shot down in front of his apartment house recently, but not by Noriega's men."

"Who then?"

"The Mexican mafia."

11

Jesse considered the ramifications of Lorraine's bombshell news. What the hell? Why was the Mexican mafia even in Panama? After trying without much luck to decide what to do with the information, including if he should tell Burt at this point, Jesse decided to temporarily shelve the fact that the trouble that killed Pablo's father reached into Mexico and perhaps the US.

Picking up the phone, Jesse started to dial, but stopped and unscrewed the mouthpiece on the phone's receiver to check for a bug. He also ran his hand under his desk and around his computer. Nothing, but he was no expert, so he made a cryptic call to a buddy in the tech department, getting the message across that he wanted his desk checked ASAP. Then he headed home.

Jesse found Pablo on the patio checking out the barrels of vegetables Clare had planted.

"You enjoy gardening?" asked Pablo.

"Not sure yet. My girlfriend is a big gardener. I keep forgetting to water, so she might demote me at any time."

"I thought I'd find you married. Is she a special *chiquita*? You know... the one?"

With all of the drama unfolding in the last few hours, Jesse forgot that Pablo and Clare knew one another.

"You know her. It's Clare Stinson. She moved to Fort Clayton at the beginning of our senior year."

Pablo's brow crinkled as he thought back. "Ah, the pretty *chica* with the red hair! Have you been together all this time?"

"No, we actually just reunited not too long ago at a Zonian party here."

"And Lorraine? What happened to her?" asked Pablo. Jesse noted how the old spark had understandably disappeared from his friend's voice.

"She stayed in Panama. Married a Marine."

"Such a beautiful *muchacha*. I always thought you would marry her."

"Things don't always turn out the way you think," Jesse said, immediately regretting his words. "I'm sorry."

"Don't apologize for my father's death. It's not your fault."

It may not be the fault of Noriega's men, either, Jesse thought, but decided not to say anything just yet.

"I thought you might want to go get some lunch."

Pablo nodded.

"There's a little burger dive down the street. The food is great," said Jesse, thinking that if the Mexican mafia shot his father, he'd better not take Pablo to anyplace too public.

Over burgers, Jesse asked Pablo about the shooting. "What makes you think that Noriega guerrillas killed your father?"

"They have always been against him. Ever since he spoke out after they sabotaged his brother's plane and sent him to his death in that accident, as they called it. My father survived a few close calls after that."

"Does the name Mendez mean anything to you?"

"No, who is Mendez?"

"Know anything about the Mexican mafia? He was the kingpin's brother."

"Was?"

"Someone killed him nine months ago."

"There seems to be a lot of that going around. Where's the connection?"

"It gets more complicated. The Italian mafia."

Pablo threw up his hands. "I know I come from a line of military leaders, but I have never understood all of this senseless killing."

Jesse shrugged. "I ask myself the same question all of the time."

Pablo and Jesse sat silent for a time, both sipping their beers.

"You know, you're welcome to stay as long as you need to. Until you can work things out," Jesse said, breaking the silence.

Pablo smiled. "You've always been a good *amigo*. That's why I came to you. *Muchas gracias.*"

Jesse watched Pablo nibble on his French fries, and then push them away, half eaten. The worst part of having his old friend around was facing the empty shell he'd become. No more wise smiles and knowing winks. Jesse vowed to sift through all of this and find out the truth for Pablo.

"Why you always in Panama? Too good for the Zone now?" Randy tossed the accusation at Jesse one Saturday night when he came to pick him up for another party at the Spinning Club.

"I'm always in the Zone, and so is Pablo. Tonight, we're cruising in Panama. Wanna come?"

"Nah, me and Sam got a lot of people expecting deliveries at the party."

"Don't get caught selling that crap."

"Okay, Mom," replied Randy. "You be careful, too. One of those crazy drivers might run you off the road downtown."

During the last year as he and Pablo became good friends, Jesse grew to like visiting Panama City. He'd been there many times with his parents over the years, but when he headed there with Pablo, he saw the area from a whole new perspective. No longer did he view the city as a far-off concept, like when he flipped through *National Geographic*. With Pablo, he felt and saw the desperation and need.

"How old are these buildings?" Jesse asked as they headed through the barrio on the way to a disco in Pablo's Corvette. The wooden structures lining the streets leaned slightly, making them appear propped up like overused decks of cards about to collapse on top of one another.

"The French threw the buildings up about 150 years ago for the workers who tried to construct the Canal," said Pablo. "As you know from history class, the first Canal construction failed terribly. Malaria killed many workers off, so they gave up. After that, you Americans got involved, and, I admit, got the job done."

An old man pushed a vegetable cart along the edge of the crowded street, most likely heading home for the night. He put his arm out to prevent the jumbled produce from falling out of the cart, which rattled along on the verge of losing a wheel. A couple of blocks later, they reached a street pockmarked by tiny liquor stores known as *bodegas*. Jesse saw several owners closing their stores for the day, pulling iron gates shut and locking them. One shopkeeper shooed away a shirtless, barefoot boy in tattered shorts and yelled at him when he outstretched empty hands.

"There is no running water in many of those wooden buildings and electricity is rare," Pablo said as he drove. "They are infested by rats and *cucarachas,* and many families live together in just one room."

"It sounds like you know it from the inside," said Jesse, trying to reconcile the wealthy Panamanian beside him with the image.

"I have. A friend lived there."

"But not anymore?"

"No, like many before him, he died from too much want—money, food, a decent place to live, medicine," said Pablo. "Gringos have lived for years in the Canal Zone, but they don't understand what it's like to be really poor with no recourse."

"I don't know where your government needs to start in order to help them, or what my government could do. Maybe it's not my business."

"It's everyone's business! The police shot my friend when he tried to steal food for his mother, brothers, and sisters."

"What a sad way to lose your life."

"He was only ten; I was eleven. We met one day on the streets while my mother shopped."

"How did that get by your mother?" Jesse asked, surprised.

Pablo grinned. "I blackmailed my bodyguard. I'd seen him sneak a maid into his room at our family estate, so when he objected to my befriending Jose, I threatened to tell on him. Eventually, when my mother did find out, she wasn't happy, of course, and didn't understand why I wanted to talk to a peasant. My parents worried I'd get diseases from such *campesinos*."

"Why did he become important to you?"

Pablo shrugged his shoulders. "We are friends with who we are friends with, no, *amigo*? He wasn't afraid of me, like so many of the kids at school, because they knew who I was. Everyone always stopped talking when I approached or let me win at games on the playground. Jose didn't know any better, and I liked that."

"I think I understand," said Jesse, imagining how hard it'd be to recognize true friends if everyone constantly tried to impress you.

A few minutes later, they pulled up to a Panamanian discothèque. Outside, neon lights flashed, promising hot dance *música* and Seco Herrerano. Pablo slid out of the car and handed his keys to a parking attendant. Running both hands over his hair as he approached the front door, he stopped in front of the stocky, muscular bouncer and flipped open his wallet to reveal a gold pass. The man smiled and stepped aside, and Pablo and Jesse entered the disco.

Once in the cool bar, the pulsating music and frenetic light display bouncing around the room unbalanced Jesse, who paused to let his eyes and ears adjust. A short, well-endowed waitress walked toward them, her breasts threatening to spill out of her white corset top with each step.

"Pablo, *mi amor, cómo estás?*" she cooed.

"I'm doing well, Marlita. *Cómo está usted?*"

"Better with you here."

"Where are they?"

"Over there," she replied, pointing a long red nail to a booth in the far right corner of the room. As they approached the table, Jesse saw two Panamanian girls.

"Pablito!" they both cried.

Leaning over the table, he kissed them each on both cheeks and then turned to Jesse.

"This is my friend, Jesse. Maria, my sister, and our longtime friend, Susanna."

Jesse sat down next to Susanna, who said in clear but slow English, "It is very nice to meet you."

Pablo took a seat next to his sister and pulled a cigarette from the pack sitting on the table.

"This is your gringo friend?" said Maria, eyeing Jesse critically.

"Be nice, Maria," Pablo warned.

She ignored her brother and asked Jesse, "*Habla español?*"

"*Si, un poquito,*" Jesse replied.

"A little is all you gringos ever speak."

Jesse made a quick assessment of Maria. Except for the giant chip on her shoulder, Pablo's sister was quite attractive. She wore a simple black dress and her dark, glossy hair spilled over her shoulders. When she looked up through thick eyelashes, her brown eyes seemed to almost glitter. Susanna, her companion, didn't have the same dark beauty, but her quick smile immediately put Jesse at ease.

After a couple of tense minutes as Maria glared at Jesse while they ordered drinks, Pablo grabbed his sister's arm and said, "Let's dance."

Jesse turned to Susanna and asked her to dance.

She nodded and slid out of the booth, and they headed for the dance floor. To the Latin pop tune filling the room, Susanna danced salsa, wiggling her hips and stepping back and forth and then from side to side. Jesse did his best to follow, out of the corner of his eye spying Pablo and Maria arguing.

When the music stopped, Jesse said to Susanna, "I've never seen you at the yacht club in the Zone. You ought to come sometime. I think you'd like the band."

"Oh, no, I could never go there," she said, her brown eyes wide.

"Why not? It's a lot of fun."

"Good Panamanian girls do not go there."

"I don't understand," Jesse said.

At that moment Pablo and Maria approached, his sister insisting that Susanna accompany her to the bathroom.

"Sorry, *mi hermana* can be difficult sometimes around non-Panamanians," apologized Pablo, giving Jesse a weak smile as they headed back to their table. "We don't talk about it, but a gringo betrayed and shamed her by getting her pregnant and then marrying a *gringa.*"

"Ouch," said Jesse. "What happened to the baby?"

"Maria went to my grandparents' house in El Valle and gave birth to a son. That's where he lives today. Susanna is nice, though, no?" Pablo said, changing the subject.

"Very nice. I'm curious, though, why did she say that good Panamanian girls don't go to the Zone?"

"Because they say that Panamanian girls who go to the Zone are called *gringettas.* That means they only go to get a gringo and trap him by getting pregnant. You can see how well that worked out for my sister," said Pablo. "But this conversation is much too serious. Let's change the subject and party."

As the two toasted the evening with their Panama beers, Pablo's demeanor changed, and he stopped talking. A tall, stunning woman had entered the disco, slow and easy as a panther in her black stretch pants and lavender tank top sprinkled with white sequins.

The girls returned and Susanna squealed, "Lilliana Ferrera is here! Isn't she beautiful?"

"Who is she?" asked Jesse as the elegant beauty kissed the cheeks of several people who greeted her.

"Only one of Peru's most famous models," said Maria.

"She's always on TV," said Susanna. "And Pablo knows her!"

Jesse looked at Pablo and raised his eyebrows in curiosity, but his friend's gaze never left the supermodel, who flashed their table a big smile as she approached. Pablo stood, and Jesse followed suit. When she reached their table, Lilliana slid into Pablo's arms. As the two embraced, and she kissed his cheeks, Jesse thought he heard her murmur, "Pablo, *mi amor.* It's been far too long."

"Excuse our rudeness," said Lilliana, interlocking her arm in Pablo's as she turned to Jesse with a broad smile and extended her free hand. "Who is your handsome friend?"

"This is Jesse McMillan. Lilliana Ferrera."

"Mucho gusto," Jesse said, taking her small, cool hand in his.

"It is a pleasure to meet you, Jesse," Lilliana replied. "It is okay if I call you Jesse? You may call me Lilliana."

"Of course," Jesse said.

As they all sat, Pablo said, "I heard you just finished a movie in Puerto Rico, Lilli. Adding acting to your many talents?"

"Si, it is nothing, Pablito," she said, leaning in to take a sip of his beer.

"Tell me about the movie," Pablo prodded.

From that moment on, Lilliana forgot about everyone but Pablo as she described the movie. Every time she got to an especially dramatic part of the story, she grabbed Pablo's arm. As Jesse watched Lilliana's adoring side glances at Pablo while she talked and his friend's eyes light up every time she touched him, Jesse wondered. Did Pablo realize the model was in love with him? Based on his reaction since Lilliana arrived, it looked like Pablo also loved her.

Engrossed in conversation, the two failed to notice Ricardo approaching, but Jesse did. He limped as he walked toward the table, a scowl on his face. The night with Lorraine flashed in Jesse's mind, and he became enraged all over again. The fury he felt threatened to reach a boiling point when Ricardo stopped and glared at Pablo and Jesse and then turned to the model.

"Lilliana, it is a pleasure as always to see you. *Mi mamá* would also want me to give you her regards."

"Thank you, Ricardo, darling. Send her my regards as well. Tell her I will visit her during my stay."

Ricardo gave Jesse and Pablo another dark look and disappeared into a nearby booth.

"I know you don't like him, but I must be kind," she whispered to Pablo. "His mother gave me my modeling start years ago when no one else gave me a chance."

Jesse and Pablo said nothing. By the grim look on his friend's face,

Jesse figured Pablo thought the same thing—how Lorraine dreamed of getting a modeling start thanks to Ricardo's mother, but got something entirely different, because she had the bad judgment to believe her son.

After lunch, Jesse returned Pablo to his condo and went back to work. Still unsure what to do with the information about who killed Pablo's father, he spent a couple of hours going through his notes, searching for any pieces of the puzzle he may have missed. Finally getting frustrated, he decided to go to the cafeteria to snack on some French fries and a soda. As soon as he returned to his desk, the phone rang.

"McMillan here."

"We need to talk."

"You calling me, Jorge. That's a switch."

"Those bullshit messages you been getting that talk about Gonzales and Panama? It's important you forget about them."

"What are you telling me?" asked Jesse.

"Burn the fucking messages and don't accept any more of them. Move on to your next story. You're done," said Jorge.

"Or what?"

"You have to ask me what? You're a big boy. You figure it out."

As if sucked out through a vortex, the newsroom din faded while Jesse stood with a dial tone in his ear, stunned at the warning in Jorge's voice. Then he spied something on his desk that made the dial tone sound like a fire alarm. A piece of paper with a bright red exclamation point. His tech friend's sign that his phone had been bugged, and was, for the moment, clean.

12

Jesse bolted out of the newsroom and to his car before Burt could smell trouble and start asking questions. Sitting in his MG with the windows up, he shivered and thought, damn California. This was supposed to be one of the warmest places to live in the United States, but as a child of the equator, who grew up without having to adjust to temperature fluctuations, Jesse felt chilled half the time—especially when the sun went down. With dusk settling around him, he started his car and waited a couple of minutes while it idled before blasting the heater.

A little while later, he found Clare on the patio of his condo planting a mass of greenery in one of his pots.

"Hi, Jesse, you look beat. Long day?" she asked, wiping her hands together to remove dirt.

"Not tired. Cold," Jesse replied.

"Want a cup of tea to warm you up?"

"I don't have any tea."

"I brought you some," said Clare, coming in from the patio, which sat just off the living room. "I love herbal tea when I'm cold. But it's not that cold. What's the matter?"

"Nothing. It's no big deal. Where's Pablo?"

"He left and said to tell you he'll be back tomorrow and not to worry." Clare assessed Jesse more closely. "Something did happen. I can tell."

"I need to put on a sweater," he said, heading for the bedroom.

Clare followed. "Is it the story?"

Jesse grabbed a sweater out of the closet and wrapped it around himself as he sat on the edge of the bed.

"I told Jorge about the notes and he told me to leave it alone, or else."

"That sounds ominous," said Clare, sitting down next to Jesse.

"Ya think?"

"Maybe it's time to hang this story up."

"It's not that simple."

"It is if you want to live."

"My name is on the Gonzales story that already published, which puts my reputation on the line. And all of this with Pablo, I feel obligated to help him figure out what happened to his dad."

"I understand wanting to help an old friend, but Pablo's father died in Panama. You aren't obligated in any way."

"He's my friend. He's always been there for me."

"I know you take your friendships seriously. I love that about you. But sometimes you just have to let things go."

"You mean you have to let people go?"

"That's not what I meant. Now you're putting words in my mouth. Where'd that come from?"

"Pablo's father didn't deserve to be shot down in the street."

"Of course not. What did you mean with your comment about letting people go? Are we talking about Randy now?" Clare put her hand on Jesse's shoulder, and he shrugged it off.

"I don't want to talk about him. Ever."

"Have you ever?"

"Stop before I say something we'll both regret," warned Jesse.

"Fine. Since we have nothing to talk about, I'm going home." Clare sprang up from the bed and marched out of the bedroom. He heard her gather her things and leave.

Jesse lay back on his bed and closed his eyes. Eventually, he drifted off into restless dreams that included a mix of Jorge wielding a gun in his face and Gonzales laughing at him.

Waking with his heart pounding, Jesse looked around his bedroom as his eyes adjusted. He had no idea how much time had passed. Getting up, he walked out to the kitchen and pulled the refrigerator open to peer inside at the sparse contents. He shut the door and smiled at the photo attached to the fridge of him and Tony posing with Goofy at Disneyland. Tony took Jesse as a surprise for his birthday last year. He said he felt sorry for him missing out on going to Disneyland as a kid, since he was "stuck in the Zone." Ironically, Jesse never felt stuck there. He felt at home —secure and settled and safe. He had meant to go back to Panama since he'd left all those years ago. There'd been opportunities, but he knew more played into it. Micky went back regularly and invited Jesse, but he always offered excuses. At the thought of his friend and a piece of home, Jesse decided to give Micky a call.

"Yo, who's this?" asked Micky.

"Jesse."

"My long-lost ex-friend?"

"Why ex?"

"You never come out and play anymore."

"Wanna party tonight?"

"You've got to be shitting me. I thought you gave it up."

"Not tonight. Wanna come over?" asked Jesse.

"Sure. Be there in a flash. Listen, I don't have any pot, but I can score some good coke if you want. Oh, sorry, forget I said that. I'll bring over a case of beer."

"Perfect," said Jesse.

"No *problemo!* See you soon."

An insistent rapping on Jesse's window at four in the morning woke him from a muddy alcohol slumber. Stumbling to open the window, he peered into the face of a wild-eyed Randy.

"They got Sam! I did just like he told me. I stayed in the car and kept the motor running and the lights off, but he never came back." The words tumbled out of his friend.

"Who's got Sam? Where is he?" Jesse asked as he helped Randy over the window ledge and into his room.

"The guads. I think," he said, referring to the Panamanian police. "Or shit, I don't know, maybe the connection. All I know is he never came back. Sam told me if this ever happened to just run."

"That's sounds like a good idea to me."

"Easy for you to say. You didn't just leave a buddy behind. What if something really bad happened to him?" Randy's chest heaved and his hands shook as he clasped and unclasped them. "I need a fucking joint."

"What you need is to calm down and tell me what the hell is going on," said Jesse.

Randy took a deep breath and continued, "Me and Sam went on a two o'clock run. It was a new supplier, and Sam didn't say anything, but he seemed kind of nervous. They wanted a kilo, but were supposed to pay big."

"Cocaine? I thought you guys stuck to pot?"

Randy looked away from Jesse.

"We started selling coke about a month ago. You can make ten times more money, and you get a lot for free."

"You can also get in ten times more trouble, and it's a million times more addicting," said Jesse. "What the hell were you thinking?"

"Look, I didn't come here for a lecture. Sam's missing, and I don't know what to do."

"Are you sure he's not at home by now?"

"I checked his house," said Randy. "He's not there, and besides, I have his car."

"What about his girlfriend?"

"He dates a bunch of chicks."

Jesse eventually convinced Randy that Sam was probably just laying low and would show up the next day. Despite Jesse's assurances, Sam didn't appear the next day or the next. After unsuccessfully trying to find him for a week, Randy took over the operation.

"What the hell are you doing?" Jesse asked, incredulous that Randy would even consider selling with Sam gone.

"I gotta keep things going while Sam's away."

"He could be gone for good."

"He'll be back," said Randy.

So Randy, who always refused to apply himself in school, took this opportunity to do just that. He became the Zone's main pot and coke connection. Jesse saw him jot down orders in a little black book and knew, because Randy told him, that he traveled downtown for the drugs, returning to the Zone to measure and package them in his car.

During this time, the date loomed for when the Canal Zone would officially become a part of Panama. While Jesse agonized about how the Zone would disappear and become swallowed up by Panama, Randy delivered the drugs, seemingly oblivious to the monumental changes occurring around them.

Randy was right about one thing. On a Monday, a month before graduation, Sam sauntered into English class, slid into a desk and looked directly at the teacher, Mr. Pringle.

"You've decided to finally grace us with your presence, Sam. I hope we haven't inconvenienced you this morning or kept you from other pursuits?"

"There was a death in my family," Sam said.

Silent up until his pronouncement, the classroom filled with whispers.

A short balding man with spectacles, Mr. Pringle cleared his throat. "Quiet down class. Sam, I'm sorry to hear about your loss. Please see me after class about the work you missed. There's a lot to catch up on before graduation."

Sam's "death in the family" happened to be a seven-week stint in a Panamanian jail. Although the news of his jail time set the entire school abuzz, no one got the full, behind-the-scenes story, except Randy.

"What happened to Sam? Did they torture him?" Jesse asked Randy one day.

"Look, Jess, Sam can barely talk about it, okay? It was a really heavy scene, and he almost didn't make it out alive."

"How *did* he make it out alive?" Jesse asked.

Randy's face clouded, and then he snapped, "Let's talk about something else, okay?"

"I won't tell anyone," Jesse assured him. "I'm just curious, that's all."

"You and the rest of the world," said Randy. "You should have heard Missy grilling me last night. Where did they hold him? Did he escape? Did they make him sleep with rats? Do they really serve bread and water?"

"Do they serve bread and water?" Jesse asked, having wondered the same himself.

"They didn't feed him anything," Randy said. "He survived on *cucarachas,* and they gave him dirty water once a day."

Jesse laughed. "Funny, Randy. Really, what did they feed him?"

"You think this is a fucking joke?" said Randy. "I'm serious. Don't ever tell Sam I told you."

"Don't worry. Not a word from me. Sorry, I didn't know it was that bad."

"The Panamanian jails are really bad. I'll never let them put me away."

When Micky arrived with a case of beer, Jesse grabbed a can and opened it before his friend could sit down on the couch.

"What the hell you been up to?"

"Not much. Just work," Jesse replied, downing half a can at once.

"I saw that article you did about the mafia guy. Heavy stuff. What're you doing now?"

"More mafia stuff." Jesse gulped from his beer. "How's work for you? Still at the print shop?"

"Yeah, but I want to leave. The asshole won't give me a raise, and Bridgette thinks she can get me a job at Irvine City Hall where she works."

"Still seeing Bridgette?" Jesse raised his eyebrows. "How's that going?"

"I don't know what the fuck I'm going to do about her."

"Why, what's wrong?"

"She said it."

"What?"

"The L word," said Micky.

"What, limp?" Jesse crooked his finger.

"Funny, asshole. She told me she loves me."

"Heavy shit. What did you say to her?"

"Nothing, really."

"I bet that went over real well."

"She started crying."

"That is bad. So, what are you gonna do?"

"I don't know. I really like being with her, and I don't want to be with anyone else. Everything was going fine until this shit. She had to make it complicated."

"They're not satisfied unless it's complicated," said Jesse. "Nothing is ever simple with chicks."

"What about you and Clare?" asked Micky. "How's that going?"

"Okay," said Jesse, pushing away feelings of guilt about their argument earlier.

"She said it yet?"

"No."

"She will," said Micky.

"Thanks for the warning. But that's the least of my problems."

"What is it? A big story?"

Jesse decided to share his dilemma, so he told Micky about the mysterious notes and Jorge's phone call.

"There's some pieces missing to this puzzle," Micky said when Jesse finished.

"What do you mean?"

"I'm no fucking brain surgeon, but I'd say you haven't been told every-thing. And Jorge and Gonzales want it that way."

"What do you think I should do?" asked Jesse.

"Fuck them telling you what to do! You're an investigative reporter, right? So, investigate."

"You're right," said Jesse. "I can't let this go. What's wrong with me?"

"You don't party enough," Micky said, handing Jesse another beer.

13

"Clare, what are you doing here?" Jesse's tongue felt thick as he struggled himself awake.

"I came to see how you're doing, but it's pretty obvious," she said, eyeing the empty beer cans littering the coffee table and floor.

He attempted to sit up, but the pounding in his head made him feel like throwing up, so he flopped back on the couch.

"This is how you deal with your life being threatened?" asked Clare.

"Stupid, I know," Jesse said, rubbing his temples.

Clare sighed and sat down on the couch next to Jesse, who even in his hungover state felt the connection with her that always balanced him.

"Look, my reaction last night was totally uncalled for," Jesse said. "I was being an asshole. I shouldn't have taken my work worries out on you. There's no excuse for it."

"It's okay. You've been under a lot of strain lately. It's none of my business how you've dealt with what happened in the past." Clare put her hand on his chest, as if to check his heartbeat. "You mean a lot to me, Jesse."

Seeing Clare with the morning light streaming in behind her from the condo's bay windows and feeling her hand rise and fall with his breathing, Jesse suddenly felt an overwhelming peace and rightness that he'd never experienced before. "You have no idea how glad I am that I went to that party and saw you," he said. "This past week and a half has been crazy with work, but I've never felt like my life was so right. I don't know if that makes sense."

Clare smiled and leaned over to kiss Jesse on the mouth. Then, her face inches from his, she said, "It makes perfect sense."

Despite his raging headache, Jesse's body responded to her nearness. He pulled her close for another kiss, this one deep and probing. When Clare motioned to pull off Jesse's T-shirt, Micky sat up from his passed out sleeping position on the floor.

"Son of a bitch, I think I'm gonna die, Jesse." Then he saw Clare. "Sorry, I didn't know you were here."

Clare's eyes flew open in surprise and her face reddened. "I didn't know you were here, either." She began to stand up, but Jesse grabbed her forearm. "Don't leave."

"I've got to get to work."

"Call me later?" Jesse asked, letting go of her arm.

Clare nodded and ducked out.

"Shit," Jesse said to no one in particular after she left.

"Killer hangover, huh?" Micky replied.

"Yeah," said Jesse, the hangover not at the top of his mind. He felt bad about embarrassing Clare. Why did he let things get that far with Micky there? What the hell was he thinking—in the middle of a bunch of beer cans? Probably better Micky interrupted them. Better to show her how he felt at a more appropriate time that involved a candlelight dinner and flowers.

Jesse lay there trying to muster the energy to get going for the day, when he recalled Micky's comment from the night before. Jorge and Gonzales clearly didn't want him poking around, so what were they hiding? Rising from the couch too quickly, Jesse stopped to steady himself on a wall.

"Where you going? There's no way in hell I can go to work today," moaned Micky. "I'm calling in."

Jesse made his way to the bathroom, where he attempted to clear his head with a cold shower. When he finished and got dressed for work, he felt a little better.

"Make me a giant mug," said Jesse, when he found Micky in the kitchen mixing instant coffee. "Thought you weren't going into work."

"That old geezer told me to come in or I'm fired," said Micky. "We got a big job due tomorrow. What happened to the good old days in the Zone when you could party all night and start partying again the next day?"

"What I miss is the warm weather," said Jesse.

"Tell me about it. Even now in the winter, the old man won't turn on the heater in the shop. I stand so close to the big printer to warm up it looks like I'm trying to fuck it."

Jesse took the mug of coffee Micky made him and wrapped his hands around it. The warmth made his fingers tingle as he took a measured sip, eager to get the steamy liquid into his body.

"This tastes like shit, Micky."

"Yeah, but it does the trick. Wait and see. You drink that whole cup, and it'll keep you flying until afternoon. Then you need a pick-me-up. If you don't want coffee, try two Mountain Dews. They're full of caffeine."

Jesse shook his head and chuckled at the hangover advice.

Micky sighed. "I just wish that frigging peanut farmer hadn't signed the treaties, and we were still in the Zone."

"You and me both."

"But you did good, yeah? At least you got an exciting job here. That wouldn't happen in the Zone."

"That's true," said Jesse, taking another sip of the raunchy liquid. So exciting it could get me killed, he thought.

When he arrived at the paper a few minutes later, Jesse walked in to find Burt chewing out Phil.

"Frigging unbelievable! You'd think this was your first day on the job. If you can't substantiate that quote, we can't use it. Call him again."

Jesse tried to slip into his chair unnoticed, but Phil saw him as Burt stalked off. Phil rolled his eyes and started to say something to Jesse, but the mail clerk interrupted when he walked up with another familiar envelope.

"Let me guess. Dropped off at the front desk like the other one? And the receptionist has no idea where it came from?"

The mail clerk nodded and continued with his deliveries.

Jesse opened the envelope and pulled out the note with the familiar loopy script.

Glad to see that you are taking my treasure hunt seriously. Now on to the next piece of the puzzle. Ever heard of el Big in Tijuana? Go there to discover vital information about who killed your friend's father. Ask for Señor Alvarez.

Cryptic, yet revealing like the other notes, this one stunned Jesse with the reference to Pablo. Any prior doubts about being watched slipped away. The author of the notes knew intimate details about Jesse's life, and the confirmation made him feel an unease that quickly morphed into a low-grade panic. He spent the rest of the afternoon making calls to find out more about el Big. He checked in with Alexa at the *San Diego Union Tribune,* and she gave him a good rundown.

"It used to be a neighborhood taco joint, but now the locals stay away. The place is a big hangout for mob bosses and their own army of informants," said Alexa. "Whenever reporters want to get the real dirt on what's happening on the streets of Mexican America, they cross the border into Mexico and go there. A lot of cops visit the place, too."

"You ever been there?"

"Plenty of times, but keep in mind that it's a hot spot," said Alexa. "If the wrong person ventures in by mistake, take my word for it, they don't stay long. There's an impressive list of mafia bosses and their entourages that have gotten plugged there. If you've got some serious shit riding on this meeting, enter through the kitchen door. The head cook's name is Arturo. Tell him I sent you."

Jesse hung up the phone and pulled out of his desk drawer the matchbook he found in the limo the night of his broken finger. La Estrella Bar & Grill was in South County, so he'd be passing by on the way back from el Big. He might as well stop in and look for the overly talkative waitress he'd been told about. Still uneasy, Jesse wondered about the wisdom of going to el Big alone. He decided to take Tony up on his offer and ask for backup.

When Jesse got home later that day, he went to Tony's condo and found him knocking back a beer on the front porch.

"What's up? Waiting for pamphlet pushers to come and save you?" asked Jesse.

"I sent them to your place," said Tony. "Want a beer?"

"No, thanks. I drank too many last night."

"I thought you just worked all the time."

"I wish I worked last night. I feel like shit."

"Bummer. How's work going, anyway?" asked Tony.

"That's what I want to talk to you about. I need backup tomorrow. Any way you can take a trip to Tijuana with me?"

"Cross the border into Mexico, huh? We finished framing a Hollywood mansion today, and I got tomorrow off. What's the plan?"

"Let's see how things unfold."

"Okay, count me in."

On the way to Tijuana the next morning, Jesse drove as Tony told him one bad construction joke after another.

"No more, Tony, I can't take it," Jesse finally pleaded.

"Okay, I'll stop if you let me in on exactly what we might get ourselves into today."

"You remember the notes from my anonymous source?"

Tony nodded.

"The note maker has been feeding me info, and it's been on-target. Last night's note said that I can get info about Pablo's dad's murder at el Big in Tijuana."

"el Big?"

"A Mexican mafia restaurant."

"You carrying?"

"You mean a gun? No," said Jesse.

"That's a stupid move. Good thing I brought mine."

"You've got a gun? Something I never knew about you, Tony."

"I don't advertise it. Too afraid some deranged chick or jealous boyfriend will turn it on me." Tony chuckled.

When they stopped at the guard booth, the border police peered several times into the car and then waved them through. Once in Tijuana, Jesse became nervous. Although Tony's presence gave him an added measure of confidence, it also alarmed him. Until now he hadn't thought through that his friend could end up in a dangerous situation, or worse. He decided to give him an out.

"Look, you don't have to do this. We can go back."

"No way, we've come this far," said Tony. "Besides, this is something you need to settle, right?"

"Yeah, I just don't want anything to happen to you, though."

"You didn't twist my arm. I'm here because I want the practice. Hopefully I'll be a detective one day."

Jesse navigated the streets of the populated border town that overflowed with pedestrians, honking, old, dented cars, and street merchants selling everything from iced fruit drinks and pastries, to cheap jewelry and decorative plates. As they crawled along in his MG and got stuck behind a bus spewing smoke at them, Jesse closed his window and vents.

"This place stinks, man," said Tony. "Was it the same in Panama?"

"In the city, yes. Not in the Zone, though. I'm not sure how they did it, but somehow they managed to keep Panama in Panama." As Jesse said this, he realized how elitist that sounded, and for the first time in his life felt a little embarrassed about the Zone.

"I think that's the place over there," said Tony, pointing to a turquoise colored wooden building with el Big painted in red across the top of the double front doors.

Jesse pulled into the gravel parking lot and parked at the back of the building. They got out of the car and headed for an open door. Feeling like a sniper had a rifle's scope pointed at him and Tony, Jesse walked at a brisk pace. In the open doorway of the kitchen stood a beefy Mexican in a stained apron smoking a cigarette. He looked to Tony for an explanation, but Jesse spoke up.

"*Esta* Arturo?"

"That's me. Who wants to know?"

"Alexa Kent told me I should make contact with you."

"Alexa, *cómo está élla?*" asked Arturo, who broke into a grin and let them pass.

Jesse and Tony entered, sidestepping a harried cook, who cursed when a batch of taco shells cooking in oil splattered grease in his face.

"Thanks for asking me to come along," said Tony. "Been too long since I got the adrenaline really pumping."

"Wait till we're home safe before you thank me," said Jesse as they left the kitchen and entered the dining area, which consisted of a number of tables and a counter containing a smattering of customers. At the back of the restaurant, Jesse noted an empty, large table where he imagined they held meetings, and behind that a closed door leading to who knew what kind of snake pit.

A young waitress approached and said in English, "May I help you?"

"I'm looking for *Señor* Alvarez," Jesse replied.

"That's him over there," she said, gesturing her head to a slender Mexican man in a blue suit, who sat at a table by himself smoking a cigarette.

"Who is he?" Tony whispered.

"Never seen him before," mumbled Jesse, leading the way.

"*Señor* McMillan. I see you brought your bodyguard. No need, we're all friends here," the man said, stubbing out his cigarette as he rose.

"That's good to know, *Señor* Alvarez," replied Jesse, shaking their host's hand.

"So how do you like el Big?" he gestured to the quiet restaurant as the waitress walked by with a tray of tortilla chips and salsa.

"Looks like a little piece of home," said Jesse, thinking how he wanted to get out of there as soon as possible. "Excuse me for asking, but I'm a little bit at a loss. An anonymous source said that I should look for you here."

"It's not I who can help you. You must come with me," said the man, who picked up his packet of cigarettes and threw a wad of pesos on the table.

"I don't get into cars," Jesse informed him.

"We are walking. It's just down the street." He pointed to the front door and headed for it.

Jesse's stomach lurched at the thought of leaving out the front, but he and Tony followed their guide. When they stepped out into the sunlight, Jesse half expected a bullet in his chest. Instead, the man led them down a narrow, potholed street. A couple of blocks later, they stopped in front of a bar with tattered orange awnings covering the two windows that flanked an open door. Jesse heard glasses clinking inside and smelled the mix of beer and cigarette smoke that seeped into the street.

"Go inside and order a drink," their guide said and walked away.

"Hey, where are you going?" Jesse called after him, but the man had already disappeared around a corner.

Jesse raised his eyebrows at Tony.

"We've come this far. Let's go." Tony turned toward the doorway and Jesse followed. Inside, the two stopped for a moment to allow their eyes to adjust to the dim light. Then they headed to the bar.

"What do you want?" Jesse turned to ask Tony.

"A Bud's okay, but if they have St. Pauli Girl, I'll take that."

"St. Pauli Girl, now you're talking," boomed a voice.

Swiveling around to face the bartender, Jesse slammed his hand on the bar when he saw who stood in front of him.

"*Chuleta*! Jesse McMillan!"

After a moment, Jesse finally exclaimed, "I can't believe it. Sam Elvia. I never expected to see you here!"

"You and me both. How long has it been since the Zone?"

"Almost ten years."

"What the hell are you doing here?" asked Sam.

"That's a long story."

14

"I'm looking for some information," said Jesse, peering around the bar to see if anyone appeared to be listening. "Can you talk?"

"Let's go in the back," said Sam, leading them toward the rear of the building after motioning to his bartender to take care of things in his absence.

Jesse and Tony followed Sam down a dark hallway, skirting around a bucket catching drips of water from the ceiling that Jesse almost kicked as they passed. From the corner of his eye, he noted the filthy walls; including one wall splattered with red that he hoped wasn't blood. Sam led them into a tiny back room containing a wooden desk and worn black linoleum flooring.

He grabbed a couple of rickety chairs from the corner of the room and pushed them to Jesse and Tony. Leaning on the edge of the desk, he crossed his arms and asked, "So what's going on?"

Sam hadn't changed much since high school, noted Jesse. Same imposing body builder physique and no-nonsense attitude.

"I don't know if you heard, but someone gunned down Pablo Sanchez's dad last week in Panama."

"I heard something about it," Sam said.

"I'm an investigative reporter for the *LA Times* now."

Sam nodded.

"I'm trying to find out who killed Pablo's father, and the trail led me here."

"Odd, since I lay low," said Sam.

"That's what I'm thinking," said Jesse, who went on to explain what had happened over the last two weeks and how they ended up in Tijuana.

"Handwritten notes, huh? Wonder if they're connected to the hangups I've been getting."

"When did they start?" asked Jesse.

"About three days ago, so the timing jives. Whoever the asshole is, he doesn't say anything—just some creepy heavy breathing." He glanced at Tony. "Hey, we're being rude. Who's your friend?"

"Sorry. Sam Elvia, Tony Molinaro."

"Nice to meet you," said Sam, who leaned over and shook Tony's hand. "Jesse and I go way back; he's good people."

"One of my best buddies," agreed Tony.

"Pablo Sanchez. Totally trippy about his old man, considering his family was one of the most powerful in Panama," said Sam. "And you. A big newspaper reporter now. I read your article on Gonzales and thought about looking you up, but I'm out of the country a lot."

"Where you travel to?"

"Perú, Bolivia, Puerto Rico. I do exporting."

"So how are things? This your bar?" asked Jesse.

"Yeah, I own this dump with a Mexican buddy. Things are good." Sam shrugged. "My old man died of a heart attack last month."

"Sorry."

"Sorry, shit, you should congratulate me. Now no worries about my mama. She refused to leave the old bastard."

Jesse remembered hearing about how Sam's father had a problem with alcohol and a foul temper.

"I want to bring her to live in San Diego soon. Panama's going down the tubes."

"That's what I'm seeing," said Jesse.

"We gotta figure out who the hell sent you to me. Something doesn't smell right, and that makes me nervous," said Sam.

"Let me know if you hear anything," said Jesse, handing Sam his card. "For old time's sake?"

"Sure, anything for a Zonian friend," said Sam, sliding the card into the pocket of his jeans. For a moment, Jesse saw the same look in Sam's eyes that he'd seen reflected in the mirror in his own. He hasn't forgotten either, he thought.

A loud crash of glasses breaking emanated from the bar area.

"Shit, sounds like I'm needed," said Sam, springing up from his half-seated position on the side of the desk. "Wait a sec. I want to give you my contact info. Back in a minute." He walked out, slamming the door behind him.

"Pretty cool guy," said Tony.

"Yeah, he always seems to walk on the dark side, but—" Yelling from the bar interrupted Jesse. He heard Sam shouting at someone and then another crash.

Tony jumped up and pulled his gun. "That didn't sound good."

"Sam's in trouble," said Jesse, adrenaline pushing all of his senses into overdrive.

"Should we go out there?"

Jesse nodded. "I'll follow you."

"I should go alone. You don't even have a weapon."

On a whim, Jesse ran to the desk sitting along the wall and whipped open the bottom drawer. Feeling around under a bunch of papers, he found what he sought. A revolver.

"How'd you know?" Tony whispered.

Jesse shrugged and pointed the gun toward the door.

"On three," said Tony, who eased open the door, waited, then headed down the hallway and into the bar.

No one in sight when they entered the room. They stopped and stood guns ready, until a moan came from the back of the bar.

"Cover me," said Jesse to Tony, making his way behind the bar. He found Sam's employee lying on the ground.

"It's the bartender," Jesse told Tony.

"He okay?"

"I think they hit him on the head, but he appears to be coming to."

"*Ay*, no," said the bartender, who sat up, holding his head in both hands. "*Se lo llevaron Señor Elvia!*"

"What'd he say about Sam?" asked Tony.

"He says they took him. Who took him?" he asked the bartender in Spanish.

"*Yo, no sé. Tenían mascarillas.*"

"They wore masks," said Jesse.

"*Quiere usted que llame al médico?*" Jesse asked the bartender if he wanted him to call the paramedics.

"*No, mi esposa, por favor. Ella es enfermera.*"

Jesse dialed the phone at the bar and handed the receiver to the bartender when a woman answered. "He wanted me to call his wife. Says she's a nurse," he told Tony.

"Who took Sam and where the hell to?" asked Tony as they waited for the bartender's wife to arrive.

"That is the question of the day," said Jesse, thinking how this shit show just turned potentially deadly.

Once the wife came to tend to the bartender, Jesse and Tony left and made their way as quickly as possible through the crowded streets to his MG waiting in el Big's parking lot. Trying not to appear too obvious, they hurried into the car, which Jesse started up.

As he steered the car onto the street and toward the border, Tony smacked his forehead. "I failed that police academy test."

"Why? I thought you did great," said Jesse.

"They could've put a bomb in your car, man."

"I never even thought about that."

"I guess there's no point in trying to find Sam," said Tony, who took Sam's revolver from Jesse's outstretched hand and stowed both of the guns under his passenger seat.

"No clue where to look, and we're just asking for trouble if we stay," said Jesse. "I'm thinking we get back home and wait for word. I can also make some calls."

The two remained vigilant as they made their way to the crowded border. A few times during what seemed like an endless wait, Jesse saw Tony start to reach under his seat, but then stop.

"Shit, I am so amped up and paranoid," said Tony, breaking the silence after the American border patrol agent waved them through and they drove onto American soil.

"You and me both," said Jesse, who noticed for the first time that his hands shook. He gripped the steering wheel extra hard in an attempt to steady them.

"Nothing's boring with you, Jesse!" said Tony, breaking the tension by laughing.

Jesse joined in and felt his anxiety ease a little as they headed north and passed the "Welcome to California" sign.

"You up to making another stop?" asked Jesse after they'd been driving for a few minutes.

"This next place as seedy as the last? Not that I'm complaining. I just want to be prepared."

"I doubt it's as bad, but I'm making no promises. It's that bar in Dana Point. It's on the way home."

"Oh, yeah, the matchbook place."

La Estrella Bar & Grill sat tucked away on a side street off Dana Point's main beach drag. They walked in to a smattering of customers sitting in booths lining the walls. Jesse and Tony headed to the bar, where they found a bartender snacking on peanuts and watching a soccer game on a television set sitting on the prep counter across from the bar.

"*Dos* Heineken, *por favor*," said Jesse.

"*Habla español?*" asked the Mexican bartender, grinning at him.

"*Si*," Jesse replied, "*Ma o meno.*"

"*Ma o meno! Usted tiene un acento de Panamá.*"

"He commented on my Panamanian accent," Jesse told Tony. "You have friends from Panama?" he asked.

"No." The bartender stiffened, his demeanor suddenly changing. "I'll get your beer."

When he returned with their drinks, Jesse tipped him a five and said, "You've got a good ear for language."

"*Si*." He smiled.

"Must come in useful in your line of work—understanding customers and everything."

He shrugged. "It helps."

"You get customers from all over?"

"Sometimes. Let me know if you want more beer." The bartender ended the conversation and made his way to the other end of the bar.

A few minutes later a curvy waitress in a white halter top and black miniskirt walked up to the bar. "Jose, I need a rum and Coke and a Bud," she said, tapping the toe of her wedge heel while she waited.

"We're looking for a waitress named Ginger," Jesse whispered. "That could be her. She likes studs, so you're on."

Tony smiled wide and called out, "Hey, beautiful, we'd like a couple of menus."

"I can do something about that," she said, reaching across the bar and walking over with menus.

When she handed one to Tony, he added, "Besides you, what's the house specialty?"

"The bacon-*Jalapeño* burger is good; so's the roast beef dip."

"I'm a burger guy," said Tony, returning his menu. "Make it medium well."

"Me, too," said Jesse, "but make it well done."

"I haven't seen you in here before," she said, giving all of her attention to Tony.

"I haven't been here before. What's your name?"

"Who's asking?"

"Tony Molinaro. And this is Jesse McMillan," said Tony, pointing to Jesse.

She kept her eyes on Tony. "Italian, huh? My name's Ginger."

"I like women with a little spice," said Tony. "How long you worked here?"

"Long enough."

"Seen a lot of people come in and out?"

"Not a lot like you," she said, leaning closer. "You looking for someone in particular?"

"I've got this Panamanian friend."

Ginger's eyes widened and she glanced toward the bartender. "I'll get your order going," she said, spinning around on her heels and heading toward the kitchen.

"Hey, we were getting along so well!" Tony called after her.

"You're doing great," Jesse assured him. "Try to get her number, or at least give her your number."

Fifteen minutes later when Ginger returned with the burgers, she asked, "You want ketchup?"

"Ketchup is good," Tony said. "So is a smile from you. I wouldn't have mentioned Panama if I thought I'd get you in such a bad mood."

Ginger gave Tony a tentative smile. "Panamanians aren't my favorite people lately."

"The news and all?"

"Just some firsthand experience with a Panamanian guy, but I'd rather not talk about it," she said in a low voice, grabbing a cleaning cloth from the bar and wiping it down.

"Sorry to interfere," said Tony, who handed her a card. "That has my number."

Ginger took the card and smiled. "I prefer the tall, dark, and handsome types," she said, finally looking Jesse's way as she slid the card in her bra. "No offense."

Jesse laughed. "None taken."

At home, Jesse found Pablo sitting on the couch.

"*Pablo, qué pasó?*"

"I went to visit an old friend from the Panamanian embassy to see what I could learn about my father."

"Anything?" asked Jesse.

Pablo shook his head.

"Did you meet him at the embassy? That might be dangerous."

"No, we met at a park. He didn't know anything, but he kept looking over his shoulder."

"That's understandable," said Jesse, sitting down in his armchair. "A pretty exciting day for me and Tony."

"*Si*? What happened?" asked Pablo, sitting up and leaning forward.

Jesse told him all about the events of the past couple of days, including the messages and how the notes led them to Tijuana and Sam, and then about his abduction.

"Kidnapped!" cried Pablo. "What next?"

A key in the lock gave Jesse and Pablo a start. The door swung open and Clare stood in the doorway. "Sorry, am I interrupting something?"

"No, it's great to see you," said Jesse, springing up.

Pablo rose, too. "Please, excuse me. I am making some tea in the kitchen." He nodded at Clare and left the room.

"At least someone is drinking your herbal tea," Jesse said.

Clare smiled and gazed out at the patio.

"I'm sorry about yesterday," he said, approaching and stopping a few feet in front of her. "I was kind of out of it and forgot Micky was here. I just—" He paused, irritated with himself. What he wanted to say pulled at his heart, but he couldn't think how to express his feelings.

Clare waited until Jesse finally managed to utter, "I don't know what got into me. Stress from the story, I guess."

"Forget it. You're entitled to tie one on now and then. I just worry about you. That's all," she said, stepping forward and sliding into his arms. Jesse felt himself melt into her soft and yielding welcome. "I've missed you," he murmured into her hair. "More than you can imagine."

Clare pulled back and met Jesse's eyes and smiled. "I've missed you, too."

He responded by taking her mouth with his.

Moments later, they heard Pablo clear his throat and pulled apart.

"I can come back," he said, setting a tray with tea cups on the coffee table.

"No, don't be silly," Clare said as she sat down in the armchair and Jesse took the space next to Pablo.

"What's the latest?" she asked, picking up a cup and welcoming Millicent onto her lap for a petting. "I know you guys have been busy, but tomorrow night is New Year's Eve. I heard about this Zonian party we could go to."

Before Jesse could answer, the doorbell rang.

"I'll get it," he said, jumping up and heading to the front door. When he put his eye to the peephole, no one stood on the stoop.

"Aren't you going to answer it?" asked Clare.

"There's no one there," he said.

"Maybe they left a package or something."

The thought of a bomb on Jesse's front porch made him yank open the door. There on the doormat lay a familiar white envelope. He reached down and picked it up, pulling the letter out and reading it.

If you ever want to see your friend from the Canal Zone again, come to 312 S. Main Street in Santa Ana tomorrow night at eight o'clock. Bring your house-guest, but no one else.

"Oh, my God, Jesse, what is he talking about?" asked Clare, who stood behind him reading the letter.

"They've got Sam. Some thugs in ski masks came in and took him when we went to his bar in Tijuana today."

"You were there!"

"In the back. Maybe they didn't know about us, or, I don't know," said Jesse, struggling to understand how the pieces all fit together.

Pablo took the letter from Jesse and read it, a deep frown knitting his brows.

"We've got to go," said Jesse.

"*Si*, they kidnapped Sam, and we must end this," Pablo agreed.

"Are you both crazy?" exclaimed Clare.

"If we don't go, Sam could die."

"Jesse!"

"I know the letter said not to bring anyone else, but I'll ask Tony if he can come as backup. We'll be okay. I promise."

"You can't promise that," said Clare.

Jesse didn't bother answering. She was right.

15

After Clare left, Jesse and Pablo sat in silence, Jesse reading the newspaper.

"They still haven't found Noriega," he commented as he scanned an article about the search efforts, but then regretted bringing up the subject when Pablo moaned, "*Ay, Dios mío,*" and put his head in his hands.

"I'm sorry, Pablo," said Jesse, folding and laying down the newspaper. "I know leaving your home is hard, believe me."

"That is true. You also left Panama," Pablo acknowledged. "But your home is here. You are an American." He gestured to Jesse's condo.

"Technically, yes, but sometimes I feel like a foreigner in the US."

"You do?" Pablo's eyes widened.

"I lost my home nine years ago. September 29, 1979. The truth is my nationality is Zonian."

"How strange life is," Pablo said. "A time of celebration and liberation for the Panamanians. But for you, a dark day."

"One of my darkest," said Jesse, recalling that bittersweet final day in the Canal Zone.

Maria's vacuuming hummed reassuringly as Jesse smoked a cigarette at the foot of the back porch stairs. She must feel pretty weird, he thought, of the woman who'd been their maid as long as he could remember. He knew she felt torn about the treaties. He'd heard her talking to his parents a few weeks back about being grateful for a good, steady job for so many years when many of her relatives struggled financially. He also understood her allegiance to her country, which would at midnight technically own his house, though they wouldn't take over the Zone right away.

At that thought, the cigarette no longer tasted appealing. Stubbing it out on the porch step, he threw it into some leaf litter under the mango tree and inhaled the sweet scent of overripe fruit. A macaw squawked overhead, and Jesse looked up at the massive tree laden with fruit the color of grenadine in a tequila sunrise. Tree leaves rustled and Jesse smiled as he searched for the three-foot iguana that had lived in the tree as long as he could remember.

Maria opened the back door. "*Chiquito*, Randy is on the *teléfono*. Come, I will make your breakfast."

Jesse climbed the stairs two at a time and went into the living room to pick up the phone.

"Does today suck or what?"

"What are you going to do afterward?"

"After what? Today's parties?" asked Randy.

"No, after the Zone changes hands," said Jesse. "Are you going to college next spring?"

"There's no point in me going to college," said Randy.

"Because you've never been a good student? It's not like you're not smart."

"CZC is a junior college," said Randy. "To really get anywhere you need to go to a university, and I'm never leaving this place."

"After the Panamanians take over the Zone, it won't be the same here anymore. If you get caught with drugs in the future, the Canal Zone cops won't be here to simply slap your hand," Jesse warned. "After tonight, the guads will sniff out drug deals and throw you in jail, like what happened to Sam."

"I know exactly what to do if I ever get caught," said Randy.

"What are you talking about?" Jesse asked.

Randy changed the subject. "You think you'll marry Lorraine?"

"I never thought about it," said Jesse. "You and Missy thinking about getting hitched?"

"Maybe," said Randy. "I know she's the best chick for me, and I only want to be with her. You know, there's a party starting at the Spinning Club right now. It's supposed to go all night."

"It's only eleven in the morning."

"So what. You don't want to go out like a wimp, do you?"

"I'll see you there later."

In the kitchen, Maria served Jesse his favorite, a pile of steaming pancakes, sided by a small, heated bowl of syrup and a glass of orange juice. She stood at the stove, starting a pot of *arroz con pollo* for dinner.

"What you going to do today, *mijo?*"

Jesse shrugged his shoulders and considered, eventually deciding after his late breakfast to take a drive to the place where he always felt at peace.

He found the Causeway deserted when he pulled onto the mile-long strip of land that shimmered in the early afternoon sun. Stopping midway, he shut off his car, then sat motionless, staring out at the water. After a time, a car drove up to the right of him. Jesse turned to see Missy.

"Are you going to the party?" she yelled out while rolling down her window.

"In a while. What are you doing here?"

"I wanted to take a drive alone and figured it'd be quiet here," she said.

"Randy at the Spinning Club?"

"Yeah. Can I talk to you about something?"

"Sure."

She got out and came to his window. "I'm worried about Randy. He's really gotten deep into coke. Can you talk to him?"

Jesse sighed. "I've tried to. He's really stubborn sometimes."

"It's just—" Missy's chin and lower lip trembled, and she looked away.

"Just what?"

She shook her head. "Nothing. I worry about him, is all."

"I'll try to talk to him tonight," said Jesse.

When Jesse arrived at the Spinning Club that evening, by the silence that greeted him, he thought the outdoor party had moved elsewhere. Then he found a throng of Zonians standing on the north edge, which faced the giant locks of the canal, watching wordless as a ship passed through. When it became clear that it was an American vessel, the silence broke and the crowd cheered and waved. The band added to the celebration by starting up, and everyone began dancing on grass that would turn to mud before the night ended. He watched Lorraine, like many others, loosen up and become more uninhibited as the beer flowed and the smell of pot filled the air. At one point, Jesse's heart clenched when Lorraine closed her eyes and swayed to the music, tears streaming down her face. She wore a short, yellow dress and danced barefoot, an emerald green Panama beer bottle clutched by the neck in one hand. Thousands of stars blinked in the sky, a bewitching sight high above the dance floor.

Around midnight, as Jesse dug a couple of beers out of the cooler next to his car, Randy ran up. Winded, he stopped to lean against Jesse's MG. "You seen Sam?" he managed to ask.

"No, why?"

"We got a run to do. Beaucoup bucks!"

"Tonight?" asked Jesse.

"It's some major coke. Can you come with me?"

"No way. I'm spending tonight with Lorraine. Let Sam take care of it."

"I can't. This is my business, too. A lot of people are waiting," said Randy. "It'll just take a few minutes."

"That crap ruin your hearing? I said no. Why don't you join me and Lorraine?" Jesse said, grabbing him by the forearm.

Randy pulled his arm away. "I gotta go."

"Randy!" Jesse called, but his friend got swallowed up by the crowd.

The next night, Clare decided to wait at Jesse's while he, Pablo and Tony went to Santa Ana to find Sam.

"I'm so sorry to leave you alone on New Year's Eve," Jesse told her. "Why don't you go to that Zonian party?"

"I'm going to be too worried about you to enjoy myself. I'll just stay here and keep Millicent company."

"I'll make it up to you," said Jesse.

Clare put her hands on his cheeks. "I'm going to make sure you do. Please promise me you'll be extra careful."

"I promise," he said, kissing her on the forehead and then leaving the condo with Pablo to pick up Tony at his unit.

Tony answered the door with the phone to his ear. "Great to hear from you, Ginger," he said, raising his eyebrows at Jesse. He grinned and then frowned. "Some important info? We're about ready to head out."

Jesse motioned to Tony.

"Wait a minute. Jesse's trying to tell me something." He put his palm on the phone's receiver.

"We need to find out whatever she has," said Jesse.

"She wants someone to go to her place in Mission Viejo. Says she doesn't want to talk about it on the phone," said Tony. "I can go and get the info, if you want, and then meet up with you guys."

"It'd be better if I went," said Jesse. "I know all of the players in this thing. Why don't you go ahead with Pablo? I won't be far behind you."

Tony returned to the phone call. "Hey, sugar, I talked to Jesse. Like I said, we've got an important meeting tonight." He paused and laughed. "Yeah, important enough to miss celebrating New Year's. Okay if Jesse comes over for that info? I'm sure it could help us. Thanks, you're a doll. Let me get your address." Tony grabbed a scrap of paper and a pen.

"You got Sam's gun?" Tony asked Jesse after he hung up the phone.

"Yeah, but you guys are going in first, so you should have it," said Jesse, handing the gun to Pablo. "Be careful."

"You, too," said Tony as they all headed out.

. . .

Ginger answered the door wearing a terry cloth robe.

"Sorry, I'm in the middle of getting ready for a party tonight," she said, letting Jesse into her apartment.

"Thanks for giving us a call," said Jesse. "What did you want to tell me?"

"You and Tony seem like nice guys, and I don't meet many nice guys, so I thought you might want to know that there could be trouble," said Ginger, motioning for Jesse to follow her to the small kitchen adjacent to the living room, where she took a sip from a wine glass. "Want anything to drink?"

"Thanks, but I need to keep my head clear for that meeting."

"Okay, I'll make this quick, so you can get going," she said. "I know your friend Rico from Panama, and he's bad news."

Jesse thought of Pablo. "My friend's name isn't Rico."

"It isn't?" Ginger seemed surprised. "That's funny, because he talked about you last night. After you guys left, he came into the bar and got hammered."

Ginger must be referring to someone else, thought Jesse. "What did this Rico say?"

"Rico's been hanging out at the bar for about six months now. I made the mistake of going out with him one night when he started coming around. He got really rough with me when he didn't get his way, so I've steered clear ever since. He definitely knows you from Panama. Last night he mentioned your name a bunch of times, Jesse McMillan."

"You said trouble. What kind of trouble?" asked Jesse.

"He kept going on and on about how he couldn't wait, because it was almost payback time. Not sure what that means, and I didn't ask."

Jesse strained to think of who she could be referring to. "What does he look like?"

"He's a short guy—barely up to my chin. Curly, black hair. He seemed nice at first, and I felt kind of sorry for him, with that limp."

Her words knocked Jesse sideways for a moment. "He has a limp?"

"Yeah, you know who he is?"

"Listen, you're a doll. Thanks for telling me this. And happy New Year's." Jesse reached into his pocket, pulled out several twenties and pushed them into her hands.

Surprise crossed Ginger's face. "Thanks, you too," she called after him as he bolted out the door and to his car.

Once on the freeway, Jesse pounded the steering wheel, berating himself for overlooking the obvious. There'd been so many signs. The familiar voice in the limo, the guy in the hotel hallway who liked to do all of Gonzales's dirty work—Rico was Ricardo! What kind of trap were Pablo and Tony walking into?

When he finally reached the address in Santa Ana, Jesse pulled into the parking lot of what appeared to be a warehouse. He quickly shut off his lights and engine, stopping next to Tony's car. They'd already gone in. Now what? Jesse got out of the MG, quietly pushing the car door shut. As he crept toward the hulking prefab steel building, he jumped a foot when a low whistle came from the shadows. Tony huddled in the bushes next to a doorway with a sign that said "office." Jesse ran over to crouch down next to him.

"Pablo told me to wait out here for you twenty minutes ago," Tony whispered. "I went around back and didn't see anyone, so it looks like everyone's inside."

"The whole thing is a setup, and I know who orchestrated it. His name's Ricardo. He's from Panama, and he's out for revenge. An old vendetta."

"Who's he after? Sam?"

"And me and Pablo. I'm going in."

"Is that a good idea if it's a trap?" asked Tony.

"I think it'll work if I distract Ricardo, and then you follow. He doesn't know you're here."

Jesse stole toward the front door, which he found unlocked. Slipping quietly inside to a front office that contained a desk and telephone, he held his breath and listened for any sounds. Only a clock ticking on the wall. He spotted a light coming from underneath a door across the room.

As he moved toward it, he heard a loud shout. Easing the door open slightly, he paused for a second, and then peered into what looked like a warehouse. His eyes swept along the concrete floor to the right, which contained several rows of floor-to-ceiling metal shelving stacked with boxes. To the left sat a variety of machinery, including a forklift, and in the center of the room he saw a figure lying on the floor. Jesse froze. Was that Sam? Pablo stood several feet from the person on the floor, his arms in the air.

A voice came over a loudspeaker: "You can't see me, but I have a clear shot of you, *Señor* Sanchez. No false moves, or I'll blow your excuse for brains all over the floor. I'm getting quite impatient at this point, though. If *Señor* McMillan doesn't show up soon, I'll shoot you anyway and leave him to clean up the mess."

Jesse entered with his hands in the air and shouted, "You want me? Here I am!"

"Finally, *Señor* McMillan has arrived," boomed Ricardo's voice. "Welcome, *amigos*, to our *fiesta* to end all *fiestas*. So nice to see that you took time out of your busy schedules to visit, *Señor* Jesse McMillan, *Señor* Pablo Sanchez, and *Señor* Sam Elvia."

"Who the hell are you, and what do you want?" yelled Jesse, deciding for the moment to hide the fact that he knew who spoke.

"Always impatient and such bad manners, *Señor* McMillan. Every question will be answered in good time. I suggest you shut that dirty gringo mouth of yours. As you can see, you are in a position to listen, not speak. And keep those hands in the air. You don't want my patience to run thin, because I can't be responsible for what happens. If you don't believe me, look where *Señor* Elvia's bad manners got him. I found it necessary to tether and gag him."

"I know who you are," said Jesse. "The coward in the limo. I recognize your voice. And I bet you wrote those letters."

"*Bueno, Señor* McMillan. You're a genius. That's saying a lot for a Zonian. And you, *Señor* Sanchez. The man who would be king. The man who has no country."

"You talk big now, but just wait until we expose you," Jesse blurted out, his mind grappling for a way to divert Ricardo so Tony could enter undetected.

"Ah! I see the wheels are turning. Are things becoming clearer?"

"Come out and show yourself, Ricardo!" Jesse yelled.

Jesse heard what sounded like clapping over the loudspeaker. "All of that work as a journalist has finally paid off, *Señor* McMillan. So you do know who I am. I'll come out in good time, but you'll never guess what I'm bringing with me."

"Your gun?" asked Jesse. "You always were good at hiding behind weapons and your mother."

"You know nothing of my mother," yelled Ricardo. "Show some respect, or I won't give you the present I brought you."

What the hell did Ricardo have with him, Jesse wondered?

"Now you aren't so quick, are you, *Señor* McMillan? Think with that tiny Zonian brain of yours."

"You're just talking shit!" Jesse shouted.

"We shall see about that," said Ricardo. A click sounded, as if he'd turned off the intercom. At that moment, Tony rushed into the room and Jesse pointed for him to seek cover amongst the rows of boxes.

Seconds later, the door on the far side of the warehouse opened and Ricardo emerged, holding Lorraine by the neck with one arm and wielding a gun in his other hand.

"Does this *puta* put things into perspective?" he asked, pushing her away from him so she stumbled forward.

Lorraine ran to Jesse, pulling duct tape from her mouth as she reached him. "He said he kidnapped you, so I got on the next plane," she cried, and then spun around to yell at Ricardo, "I don't understand. Why are you doing this?"

"Why are you doing this?" Ricardo mimicked in a falsetto voice. "Another genius Zonian is with us. Haven't any of you half-wits figured out why you're here yet?"

Lorraine sucked in her breath and cried, "Oh, my God."

"The cockteaser remembers how she lost out on a true man!" Ricardo waved the gun around as he limped toward them, stopping several feet in front of Pablo. "I'm going to kill you like I killed your father. You shouldn't have stuck your nose into gringo business."

"*Pendejo!*" Pablo yelled, lunging at Ricardo, but Jesse and Lorraine pulled him back by the arms.

"I'm the one with the gun," Ricardo sneered. "You're the one who's going to die. And the *puta*, who should have put out, and the journalist with the big mouth. Unfortunately, I can't kill you, Sam, the not-so-big man now. Gonzales has a score to settle with you, half breed, leaving his brother shot in a parking garage like a dog. You're a traitor, working for the Italians, even though your *mamá* is Panamanian."

"You set this entire thing up from the beginning, Ricardo!" cried Jesse.

"Maybe you have more than half a brain. It's a shame; we could have been great *amigos*, you and I."

"We could never be *amigos*. I don't call rapists my friends," said Jesse.

Ricardo's face contorted in rage. "She wanted it. I was being a man. And what did I get? Broken legs."

Jesse spied Tony emerging from among the boxes and knew he must keep Ricardo's attention.

"What went wrong, Ricardo? You had a good life in Panama. Why come here to live like this?"

"You know nothing about my life, gringo!"

"Seeing what you've done now, I know you've been consumed with the need for revenge. That's no way to live, *hombre*."

"Now you call me *hombre*? How do you know what is best for me?"

Jesse searched his mind for a reply that would keep Ricardo interested as Tony continued to approach from behind. He wished he had kept Sam's gun rather than give it to Pablo. He might have been able to use it to neutralize the situation.

"You're right. We should have given you a chance, Ricardo. I know our clique was pretty tight in Panama."

At the brief flash in Ricardo's eyes, Jesse knew he'd hit the mark.

"None of you ever gave me the time of day!"

"Like I said, we should have invited you into the group," said Jesse. "That was our fault."

Tony appeared right behind Ricardo when the madman sensed him and whirled around, shooting and missing. Unfazed, Tony kept his gun steady and pointed at Ricardo's face. "Shoot again, and you're going down."

"You think I'm afraid to die?!" Ricardo yelled at Tony. "Pull the trigger and find out that I'm not."

"Forget about him, Ricardo. You want me," Jesse interjected, seeing from the corner of his eye Pablo take advantage of the commotion and run over to free Sam.

"*Cállate la boca*," Ricardo yelled at Jesse. "You've always talked too much. And you didn't follow instructions like a good little gringo. I said no *amigos*. Your friend dies, and then the rest of you."

"Why bother with him?" asked Jesse.

"You think I'm *estúpido*? He's seen everything. I don't leave any loose ends. Just ask my associates!"

Jesse watched in helpless horror as Ricardo's finger engaged the gun's trigger. When a shot rang out, it felt like Jesse's heart seized in his chest, until he saw Ricardo slump to the floor with a look of stupefaction on his face. Lorraine started to scream when blood began oozing from a hole in the side of his head.

Sam walked up and stood over Ricardo's body as the blood spread on the concrete floor.

"Glad you untied me and gave me my gun," he said to Pablo. "Another minute and this lunatic would have killed us all." Sam used his shirt to carefully wipe his and Pablo's fingerprints off the gun and then set the weapon down next to Ricardo's lifeless form.

Someone must have heard the shots and called the police, because sirens began wailing in the distance.

"Get out of here," said Jesse to Tony. "This is our mess—and being here could mean you don't get into the police academy."

"He's right, man," agreed Sam, who picked up Ricardo's gun and handed it to Tony. "Take that with you. The only gun we want on the scene is the piece that killed Ricardo. The story is going to be that he took us by surprise with it."

143

Tony left with the gun.

"It's important we get our stories straight," said Sam as the sirens got closer. "Ricardo called us, claiming he was holding Lorraine hostage. We thought he was just upset, so we came to talk him down. He had a gun, and we all scuffled. Somehow, he got shot. All four of us repeat that story, and they won't be able to pin it on anyone. You all with me?"

Pablo and Lorraine nodded.

"If they do a gun residue test, they may find some on me. I belong to a shooting range, and I went yesterday morning, so I can use that as an excuse, but I'm going to go scrub my hands and arms right now before the cops get here to try and prevent that from happening."

Jesse reminded himself that Sam probably knew best about these kinds of things and called after him as he headed to a utility sink in the corner of the warehouse, "What about your gun? Can't they pin that back to you?"

"No, I got it a couple of months ago, and that's the first time I ever used it. The serial numbers are also ground off, so it's untraceable."

Dazed at the events of the last few minutes, Jesse eyed Ricardo lying on the floor in his own blood and listened to Lorraine's sobs. This certainly wasn't the first crime scene he'd seen since becoming an investigative journalist, but it was the first one where he stood at the epicenter.

"Hell of a New Year's," he said to no one in particular as the sirens approached.

16

After two hours of questioning at the warehouse, which involved each of them sharing their own detailed accounts of what occurred, the police released them.

"We've got a little dilemma," said Jesse when they walked out into the parking lot. "I can only squeeze me and someone else into my MG."

"I made a call. Someone should be here to pick me up any minute," said Sam. As if on cue, a limo drove up and stopped by the curb. He turned to Jesse. "You going to write about what went down tonight?"

"Yes, I've been covering this whole thing for weeks."

"Nothing to do with me, right? Ricardo was always wacked. Total accident, like we told the police."

"Right," Jesse said. "Take care of yourself."

"You always were cool, McMillan," Sam said, ducking into the limo and speeding off.

"Looks like Lorraine's going to have to sit on your lap," said Jesse to Pablo, who shrugged and got into the car. Without protest, Lorraine sat down on Pablo's lap, and then Jesse started the car and headed out of the lot.

They made their way in silence, until Lorraine spoke.

"I am so sorry for all of this. When I look back, all I thought and cared about was modeling, modeling, modeling."

"We were young, Lorri," Jesse said, putting his hand on her shoulder. "All I thought about back then was being a famous writer. That's what teenagers do. They dream."

"And now look at the nightmare," said Lorraine.

"It's over, and we're all okay." Jesse hesitated. "You are okay, Lorri, right? He didn't hurt you in any way, did he?"

"No, I'm okay. He just ranted and raved about finally getting his revenge. I think he had officially lost his mind."

"Now I know who killed *mi papá*. A madman," said Pablo.

When they pulled into the condo complex, Tony came out of his unit and ran down the stairs to meet them as they got out of the car.

"I wasn't sure if they'd release you guys. They hold Sam?"

Jesse shook his head. "No, they let us all go, although they probably won't let go of it that easy. Someone picked up Sam in a limo."

"That guy travels in style, huh? You guys must be beat. I know sleeping space is limited, so Pablo can crash at my place tonight."

"That'd be fantastic," said Jesse. "Thanks a million."

Jesse and Lorraine wearily trudged up the steps to his condo, where he pulled his keys out of his pants pocket and unlocked and opened the door. He entered and Lorraine followed right behind him.

"You're okay! I was so worried," said Clare, springing up from the couch, but freezing when she saw Lorraine.

"Clare, you're still up," said Jesse.

"Of course, I'm still up! I've been sitting here terrified out of my mind, and you're off somewhere with Lorraine, who you said you hadn't seen in ten years!" Clare tried to push past them, but Jesse stopped her.

"Damn it, Clare. A lot has happened," he said. "We need to talk."

"I'll go to Tony's. I'm sure he can put me up for the night. That way you guys can talk," said Lorraine.

"No, Lorraine, stay," said Jesse.

"Yes, by all means, stay. I'm leaving," said Clare.

"At least give me a chance to explain," Jesse said.

"It's all crystal clear!"

Lorraine walked to the front door and opened it, crossing the threshold and turning around before closing the door behind her. "A lot happened tonight, Clare. Please let him explain."

Jesse watched Clare get her purse, and the night's pent-up tension flooded his words. "Please. Just give me five minutes."

Clare slung her purse to the floor and sank down on the edge of the couch. "I can't do this anymore, Jesse."

"What?" Jesse had never seen Clare like this before. When she looked up at him, the anger in her eyes told him he had better back up and listen —intently, as something was about to change here.

"I can't be a part of this forever love triangle. I just can't. That night. In the Zone. You and Lorraine, after you and I…." Clare was becoming more upset. "That felt like someone stabbed me in the heart."

Jesse felt his own heart suddenly pounding in his ears. "I'm so sorry, Clare. It's a long story. You don't know how many times I've wished through the years that I'd handled things better."

"How long could the story be, Jesse? After all these years, don't you think I deserve to hear the story? Even if it is that you loved Lorraine then and you do now? You could have been honest with me. I get it, you and Lorraine go way back, but why continue to string me along—even now?"

"That night you saw us together at the beach…." Jesse stopped, struggling to find the right words. He knew everything hinged on what happened next. "I don't know if you remember Ricardo Montego? His mom owned the Hermosa Modeling Agency in downtown Panama City. Ricardo tried to rape Lorraine that night and would have, except Pablo and I heard her cries."

Clare gave Jesse an incredulous look. "Of all the things I thought you might say. Why didn't you tell me?"

"I wanted to tell you, believe me, but Lorraine swore me to secrecy. Everything in me wanted to run to you when you saw us, but what could I say without breaking Lorraine's trust?"

"I understand that she wouldn't want people to know. I just wish I'd known."

"You know now," said Jesse. "Hopefully that helps a little."

Clare sighed. "So what happened tonight?"

Jesse hesitated.

"No secrets from now on, Jesse, no matter what."

"I don't want to make you an accessory after the fact, I think they call it," Jesse said.

"You're scaring me. What happened?"

"It turns out that Ricardo has been behind this whole thing. He wanted revenge for getting his legs broken by Sam, because of Lorraine. He was the guy in the limo who had my fingers broken, and the note maker. Ricardo lured Lorraine here by telling her I'd been kidnapped, and he also abducted Sam from Tijuana. You saw the note that told us to go to the warehouse tonight. When I got there, he had Sam tied up and Pablo standing there with his arms in the air. Then he announced he had a visitor and brought out Lorraine. He planned to shoot all of us, but Sam. He said Gonzales wants him, because Sam killed his brother for the Italian mafia. If it wasn't for Tony and Sam, we might all be dead."

"How terrifying for all of you! Oh, Jesse, if anything had happened to you." Clare got up from the couch and went to him.

He took a deep breath. Forget the champagne and candlelight. Jesse wanted to say this right here, right now.

"I don't want to talk about that anymore. I want to talk about us. I love you, Clare. I know now I always have. Since that first day I met you on the Causeway. There's no one I want to be with but you."

Clare's eyes welled with tears. "I've wanted you to say that for so long. I've always loved you, Jesse." She leaned in to kiss him on the mouth, and he responded by crushing her tight against him. When they came up for air, he murmured, "How about we take this to the bedroom?"

"A question first," she said, pulling back slightly. "Why are you protecting Sam? He killed someone, and now you're all involved."

"I owe him. For one thing, he probably saved Tony's life."

"You don't owe him anything. You didn't ask him to punish Ricardo for what happened to Lorraine by breaking his legs. That's on him. If anything, he owes you for what happened to Randy."

Jesse stiffened. "I thought I made it clear I don't want to talk about that."

"You made it perfectly clear. So clear, in fact, that subject is a wall between us."

"It wouldn't be if you would stop bringing him up."

"Pushing what happened down is keeping you trapped in the past, Jesse. You said it yourself. You've lived stateside almost a decade, and you haven't truly settled here. It's not just because you lost your home in the Zone. You know it runs deeper than that. The truth is we can't talk about our future until you deal with your past. I want all of you, Jesse, every little piece. The good, the bad—everything."

Clare picked up her purse.

"What are you doing?"

"I'm going home. It's been a long day for both of us."

"It's late. Stay," Jesse said, reaching out and pulling her to him, burying his face in her hair.

"I think you need to be alone," she said quietly.

"I'm sick of being alone," Jesse said. "You never get in the way, and besides, I'm closing this chapter of my life. It's all behind me."

"Oh, Jesse," Clare said, pulling her head back and looking into his eyes as she traced the side of his stubbly cheek with her forefinger. "It'll never be behind you until you face it head on." And then, just like that, she walked out the door.

Standing in his living room, Jesse heard the sharp sound of her heels on the pavement and her car start and head out of the complex, which made him feel utterly alone.

When the phone rang, he thought about not answering it, but finally picked it up.

"It's me, Lorraine."

"You settled at Tony's?"

"Yes, did you work things out with Clare? I thought I heard a car leave."

"I'm working on it."

"I'm sorry to cause so much trouble."

"It's not your fault," said Jesse. "None of it."

"Who would have thought Ricardo would hold such a grudge?"

"He was an evil, sick dude. Get some sleep, Lorri."

"You too," she said.

But sleep escaped Jesse. Instead, he lay in bed thinking for the first time in years about the morning that he and Lorraine said goodbye to the Zone.

In the early morning hours of their last night as Zonians, Jesse and Lorraine danced alone at the Spinning Club. When the final musician left standing finished off a bottle of beer, let out a belch, and slumped down next to his drum set, they headed for Jesse's MG, parked behind one of the welding buildings.

Once they slid into the car and sat down, Lorraine whispered, "It's morning."

Jesse turned to gaze at Lorraine, a knot of emotion in his throat. A lone tear trailed down her cheek and hung onto her chin until she wiped it away with the back of her hand.

"I can't believe it's over, Lorri. The Zone is gone forever."

She nodded.

Jesse took Lorraine's hand in his and they watched as the sun sent up faint rays of light from the horizon—the sky gradually painting itself a brilliant orange.

After two hours of tossing and turning in bed, his mind bouncing from what happened in the warehouse to that final morning in the Zone, the rain tapping on the condo roof sealed the deal for Jesse. He got up and threw on jeans and a T-shirt. Downstairs, he grabbed his keys from the table and pulled open the front door, wishing for a muggy blast of warm air. But this wasn't Panama. It was California. The raindrops that splattered his face and body when he closed the front door and made a mad dash for his MG weren't warm, but how good the rain felt after months of clear blue skies and occasional wisps of barren, uncooperative clouds.

Jesse drove to the Santa Ana foothills and headed down one of the few rural roads left in the area. Opening the window, he let the brisk air blow in to clear his head, but that didn't stop the memories that rushed at him like a monkey stampede.

"Jump," Randy had yelled up at Jesse that time so long ago as the tropical rain pounded the water's surface. They were at what all their friends called the "slide," a quarry outside of Panama City with a fifty-foot drop to the water. Jesse could barely see Randy bobbing around below.

"Chicken!" Jesse thought he heard his friend call up to him, the words a deep, hollow sound as the onslaught of rain roared throughout the quarry.

If Randy can do it, so can I, Jesse coaxed himself, while trying to ignore the fact that his heart seemed to pound harder than the rainstorm. Taking a deep breath, he stepped off the stone ledge and plummeted into the quarry. The steep, vertical plunge beneath the water seemed to cause his throat to fall into his stomach. Finally, he surfaced, gasping for air.

"All right, Jess!" Randy laughed, seemingly oblivious to the torrent of raindrops pounding his head and face. Jesse always envied how Randy could be so agile and carefree.

The rain began to beat down even harder, and Jesse panicked. The quarry had been known to rise quickly, and people had drowned down here.

As he always did, Randy sensed his friend's fear and secured his arm around his neck. "Don't worry. I'm here. I won't let anything happen to you."

But in the end, when it really counted, Jesse hadn't returned the favor. That morning when the Zone ceased to exist, as Jesse and Lorraine headed out of the Spinning Club after watching the sunrise, Micky pulled in and stopped them.

"Jesse, everyone has been looking for you guys! It's Randy. He's at Gorgas Hospital. I don't know what happened—."

Jesse didn't reply to Micky, but instead peeled out of the parking lot and sped off to Gorgas, all the while cursing himself.

"Randy tried to get me to go on a drug run with him last night, but I said forget it," he told Lorraine. "I should have stopped him."

"He has always been unstoppable. You know that. Remember in first grade when he talked us into taking a trip to the Atlantic side of the Zone all by ourselves? Our parents ran around the Pacific side looking for us all day while we played on the beach. They grounded us for what, three months? Randy thought it was all worth it."

At the hospital emergency room, they found Missy pacing in circles.

"What happened?" Jesse asked.

"He got chased by the guads and crashed his car," said Missy, her eyes swollen from crying. "They've been in there so long! Please let him be okay!"

Watching Missy pace made Jesse feel dizzy with fear. He wanted to take her by the arms and stop her. If he could just sit her down, it might calm the anxiety threatening to overwhelm him.

Randy's parents came rushing into the waiting room.

"We just heard Randy was in an accident," said his father. "We thought he was with you and Lorraine, Jesse?"

"For a while, but he left," Jesse said, a feeling of guilt washing over him as he glanced at Lorraine. She stood still, eyes on the floor.

The emergency room door opened, and a doctor emerged.

"Are you Mr. and Mrs. Strickland?" he asked Randy's parents.

"How is he?" said Randy's mother.

"The injuries from the accident weren't that bad, but your son experienced complications. Can you please sit down?" the doctor asked, pointing to chairs along the wall. Jesse, Lorraine and Missy waited while the doctor spoke to Randy's parents in a low voice.

"A heart attack! My son's only eighteen years old." Mrs. Strickland collapsed into the arms of Mr. Strickland and began sobbing.

The doctor waited until she quieted. "We believe your son ingested a large amount of cocaine. We made the discovery after he experienced the coronary, which was massive. I'm sorry, but we couldn't save him."

Missy turned ashen and Jesse helped her sit down. "He swallowed his delivery," she hissed. "Sam taught him never to get caught by the guads with his hands full."

The outside glass doors slid open and Sam rushed in.

"Where's my little buddy?" he asked breathlessly.

"Where is he?" screamed Missy, running to Sam and pummeling her fists against his chest. "He's dead. He went to pick up that horrible stuff for you, and he swallowed it because you told him to. And now he's gone. You miserable asshole!"

"Shush," Jesse heard himself soothing Missy, pulling the sobbing girl off of Sam. Despite the cold fear and denial lurking right underneath, he held her to him and talked in a soothing, low tone to calm her, watching over her shoulder as Sam sunk into a chair, the shock on his face eventually morphing into a concrete mask.

Over the next several weeks, Jesse stayed unruffled. Like an emotional zombie at Randy's funeral, he honored his best friend by talking levelly and lovingly about him during the memorial service. Then he and his parents packed the house and left Panama for California.

Now here on the open road driving at eighty miles an hour, Jesse pounded his steering wheel and yelled to an empty car, "You promised you'd be okay!"

And then things became perfectly clear. Clare had been right to go home and leave Jesse to face reality. This time he wouldn't be intimidated or afraid. This time he wouldn't hide what happened in order to spare anyone. This time he'd face his own truth. He had loved Randy, but Randy had been his own person. Jesse would honor that...finally.

17

When he got home from his drive, Jesse sat down at his computer and started writing, the words pouring out of him like the rain flowing from the sky outside.

On a quiet street in a Santa Ana warehouse last night, a man died of a bullet wound to the head. That he was a member of the Mexican mafia and killed by a rival gang is not where the story begins. Instead, it started thirteen years ago in a quiet, tropical paradise called the Canal Zone. There, under perpetually sunny skies and along palm-tree lined streets, a group of high school kids started a game of drug running that would eventually become fatal....

Jesse stayed at the computer through dawn and into the following day. At some point, Pablo came and went. Except for refueling with coffee and a sandwich, Jesse kept working on the article until he felt completely satisfied with the writing. Finally finishing in the early evening, he took a deep breath, printed it out and faxed it to Burt. Then he went to his bedroom closet and reached up, groping for the framed photo he'd put on the top shelf when he moved in several years before.

He blew off the dust and smiled at the picture of him and Lorraine flanking Randy when they were in high school. They stood on the Causeway at midday, the sun in their eyes. Lorraine scowled into the sun as she tried to shade her eyes with her hands, while Jesse squinted. Randy wore a huge grin and sunglasses, which made it easier for him to put a set of rabbit ears behind both of their heads.

Jesse stood there gazing at the photo, recalling the good times the three of them enjoyed and saying a silent goodbye, when the phone rang.

"Jesus, McMillan. This is heavy stuff," said Burt. "Can you stand behind every word?"

"Yeah. Can you print it?"

"I'm having legal look it over right now. If all passes muster, it'll hit the streets tomorrow morning."

"So, what do you think?"

"It's dynamite." Burt remained uncharacteristically silent for a moment. "Good work. You've become a topnotch journalist. Sorry about your friend Randy."

"Thanks."

"And happy New Year's. You've been through hell and back these last few days. Get some rest."

"I will. Happy New Year's to you, too, Burt."

Jesse hung up the phone and walked into his bedroom, flopping onto his bed and closing his eyes to slip into a peaceful sleep for the first time in weeks. He didn't stir until six o'clock the next morning when he awoke to the sound of the next-door neighbor's dog barking at the paperboy. After sitting up and stretching, he went out into the crisp morning and picked up the *Times*. His article took up much of the front page.

MEXICAN AND ITALIAN MAFIA AT ODDS

Gang Warfare Dates Back 13 Years To Canal Zone, Panama School Yard

He made himself a cup of instant coffee and sat down to read the article. When he finished, he thought, Burt was right. It was a dynamite story. Too bad the article spotlighted the death of his best friend. Now the thought of being rewarded for the story hardly seemed to matter anymore. He'd easily give up a chance at a Pulitzer to have his best friend here with him.

When Jesse walked into the newsroom later that morning, several reporters bombarded him with congratulations on the article, including Phil, who handed him a sealed envelope.

He recognized the writing immediately—Sam's boxy print. Running a finger beneath the flap, he opened it.

I didn't know you had it in you, McMillan. Now I know why my little buddy raved about you. I should kill your ass for bringing me up. Even though you used a pseudonym, they know who I am. But I'm not going to bother you, because I know Randy's watching me right now. You won't hear from me again. I'm going underground. Watch your back. I can't make any promises about Gonzales.

Jesse folded the note up and stuck it in his pocket when someone tapped him on the shoulder.

"Lorraine. What are you doing here?" he asked, surprised, grabbing her in a big hug.

"Tony dropped me off on the way to a job," she said, returning the hug. "The article's absolutely brilliant."

"Thanks. Burt said the publisher loved it. He wants to try to get the story on *60 Minutes*."

"Wow, that would be fabulous, so why aren't you smiling?" The question in Lorraine's eyes soon turned to understanding when Jesse replied.

"I wish the biggest story of my career wasn't about the biggest loss of my life."

"Is it possible to talk?" asked Lorraine.

"Sure," Jesse answered, searching her face for a clue as to what she wanted to discuss. "There's a coffee place on the corner."

Neither said a word until they sat down at the coffee shop.

"So, is the coffee pretty good here? Or should I go with tea?" Lorraine asked.

"I think it's safe to order the coffee. Everyone from the newsroom comes here—although now that I've said that it might not be a good idea to take the word of sleep-deprived journalists."

Lorraine laughed. "Maybe I'll get some tea."

"Thanks for not bothering me yesterday while I was writing," said Jesse as the waitress approached.

"No problem. I slept most of the day, and then Tony kept me amused the rest of the time with his stories about constructing houses for crazy rich people in Hollywood."

Jesse chuckled.

After they ordered, Lorraine fiddled with the spoon and napkin the waitress had set on the table and finally said, "I pushed that morning when Randy died out of my mind for a long time. After you left the Zone, I started partying hard and trying to forget about losing Randy, you, and our home. It's hard to explain, but the past all became blurred for me."

"I did the same thing when I moved here—immersed myself in going to school and becoming a journalist until our life in the Zone seemed like a dream. And in many ways it was," said Jesse. "Of course, we had trouble and even tragedy, but I haven't experienced anything here like the complete safety and security of living in the Zone in what was a tropical paradise protected day and night by the CZ police. You hear people say that they didn't appreciate a place or time until they lost it; but I think that's the difference for many of us Zonians. We knew what we had in that time and place, and it knitted us together forever. We appreciated each and every minute we spent with one another in the Zone, and I think that's what made it so hard to lose."

"Wow, I've never thought of it quite like that, but you're right. You've always been a master at description."

"I should have gone with him that night."

"He made his own choices. You've got to let it go. You weren't his keeper. You were his friend, and a good one."

Jesse sighed.

"I've missed you," said Lorraine.

"Me, too," said Jesse.

"We should have kept in touch."

Jesse thought about how awkward and painful the silent avoidance of Randy would have been. "I guess we weren't ready."

Lorraine nodded. "What about Sam?"

Jesse reached into his pocket, pulled out Sam's note, and handed it to her.

"You believe him?" she asked, returning the letter to Jesse.

"Sam has never been a liar."

"That's true."

"What are you going to do about living in Panama?" he asked her. "It'll be 1999 before you know it, and the military will be clearing out. Safety could become an issue after that."

"Panama's my home. It's in my blood, no matter how bad it gets. Kurt has another year of his tour with the Marines, and then we're thinking about moving to the Interior. It's really peaceful there, and pretty safe. I think we'll do some farming. He grew up on a farm in Idaho."

"The former would-be model a farmer! As long as it's not peanuts."

"Never peanuts! You're welcome to visit. I know you'll like Kurt."

"Well, you've always had good taste."

Lorraine smiled, and then said suddenly, "Hurry up and finish your coffee. I've got a surprise for you. Can you drive us to Santa Monica?"

"What's in Santa Monica?" asked Jesse.

"If I tell you, it won't be a surprise. Can you?"

"You sure I'm going to like it?"

"I know you will."

"What the hell. I'm star reporter for the day," he said, downing the rest of his coffee.

On the hour-long ride to Santa Monica, Jesse couldn't get Lorraine to spill anything about the mystery destination, so when they arrived on a street lined with magnolias, he walked up the steps of a townhome, bewildered and curious.

Lorraine knocked on the door and turned to grin at Jesse. "Trust me. This is going to make your year."

When the door opened, Jesse stared at her shocked. The years had put weight on her short frame, and she had dyed her hair red, but it was definitely Missy.

"Jesse!" she cried, putting her arms out to embrace him.

Just then Jesse heard a young boy's voice. "Mom? Is it Tommy?"

Missy moved to let them in, and Jesse stopped short in the doorway. A miniature Randy stood in the center of the living room.

"These are some friends of your Daddy's," said Missy, putting her arm around Jesse's waist.

"Yay!" the boy shouted.

"This is my son, Little Jesse," said Missy.

"Jesse?"

"It was the name Randy wanted," Missy said softly.

Jesse grabbed Missy and buried his face in her hair. When he let go, the tears that had threatened since he'd written the story spilled onto his cheeks, and he wiped them away with his fingers.

Missy looked up at him with understanding. "I found out the day before he died, and I told him."

"I didn't know," said Jesse. "I should've found you and made sure you were all right. I think the pain of losing him numbed me for a long time."

"I didn't want to be contacted," said Missy. "After Randy died, I was so mad at everyone and everything. I moved here to live with my dad and stepmom and had Jesse. It seemed far enough away so that I could forget. And I did for a while. I got a degree and moved out on my own. But as Jesse grew, and I watched other kids with their fathers, the anger resurfaced. I finally had to face the fact that though others were involved, Randy made his own decisions, and those decisions killed him. Nothing me, you guys, or even Sam could have done would have made a difference. Once I accepted that fact, I could concentrate on Jesse, and I know I've got the best of Randy in him."

All eyes fell on the boy, who studied everyone thoughtfully and then said to Jesse, "You're my dad's best friend, huh? That's why our name is the same."

"That's right," said Jesse, who walked over to the boy. "How old are you?"

"Nine. I play baseball."

Visions of Randy at nine filled Jesse's head. The same freckles sprinkled across the boy's stubby nose. The same blue eyes and long lashes.

"I knew your father when he was nine. He played baseball, too."

"What else did you play together?"

"Your dad and I built a fort once, in my mango tree."

"What's a mango tree?"

"A tree with big, juicy fruit on it. And you'll never guess what lived in the tree and ate the fruit. A giant lizard that's called an iguana."

"I wish I had a fort!"

"Maybe you can come visit sometime, and I'll show you pictures of the fort."

"Can I, Mom?" The boy looked at Missy.

"I think that would be great," she said. "Does anyone want iced tea?"

"Iced tea sounds good," said Lorraine.

Lorraine and Missy went to the kitchen, leaving the two Jesses alone.

"Come see my room," the boy said, charging into the back of the townhome with Jesse following. Little Jesse ran around to show off his toys, and the room filled with the same raw energy and excitement that Randy had once given off.

"The blue one always wins," said Little Jesse, who had picked up two remote controls for a car race and sent them speeding along the tracks. The blue one did soon overtake the green car and win the race.

Jesse reached for a control and said, "Race you?"

Little Jesse handed a control over. "You know how to play good?"

"Really good."

Lorraine walked in and handed Jesse an iced tea. "He's a charmer like his dad. Can you believe how much he looks him?"

"It's uncanny," said Jesse.

"My dad was really good looking," said Little Jesse. "My mom said so."

Jesse and Lorraine laughed.

Missy invited Jesse to stay the night, and he agreed. He and Little Jesse raced cars and looked at comic books, and he answered the boy's many questions about his father. After Jesse read him countless bedtime stories, and he finally dozed off, he, Lorraine and Missy reminisced about their days in the Zone, and especially about life with Randy.

"Remember the time he started playing around with that boa constrictor in the jungle?" said Missy. "I freaked out so bad about it wrapping around his neck and squeezing the life out of him, but he just laughed."

"And the amount of mayonnaise he piled on his fries," said Lorraine.

"Want some fries with your mayonnaise!" they all said in unison and laughed.

Jesse left the next morning, promising to take Little Jesse to a baseball game the following weekend. He hugged the boy and Missy goodbye, and then turned to Lorraine.

"I guess this is goodbye for a while," he said.

"For now. I'll be back to visit, and you're always welcome to stay with Kurt and me in Panama. Let me walk you to your car."

When they got to his MG, Jesse thanked her. "It meant a lot to me to meet Little Jesse and see Missy. You know me inside and out, don't you, Lorri?"

"I do." She smiled and then looked toward the magnolia trees that rustled in the breeze. "You're in love with Clare, aren't you?"

"Yes."

"She's good for you."

"I don't know if she wants me," he said.

"She wants you. Who wouldn't?" She smiled at him, her eyes shiny with tears.

They embraced and promised to keep in touch, and then Jesse drove away, watching Lorraine standing on the curb in his rearview mirror.

When he got back to his condo, Jesse found Pablo sitting in the living room sipping tea.

"*Amigo*, there you are," Pablo greeted him. "I'm not sure if you heard the good news, but they caught Noriega. His reign of terror is over, and my country can heal now."

"Wow, no, I didn't hear. Today?"

"Yes, I saw it on the news a few minutes ago. All of Panama is rejoicing." He raised the tea cup and took a sip.

"That's great news for you and your mom and sister. Did you tell them about your father?"

Pablo's face fell. "*Sí*, I told them yesterday, once I knew the truth about who killed *Papá*. *Mi mamá*'s heart is, of course, broken, but she has my sister, my grandparents, and my nephew there in Peru with her. Soon I will also be there."

"In Peru? Will your family stay there or go home to Panama now that Noriega is gone and you know that Ricardo shot your father?"

Pablo shrugged. "I am not sure if they will go back to Panama, but I am staying in Peru."

"You are?" Jesse asked, surprised.

"*Sí, mi amigo*, I took your advice."

"My advice?"

"Don't you remember, you told me once back in Panama that if two people are in love, there is always a way to be together? We found a way."

"That's great, Pablo. You and Lilliana?"

"*Sí*," he said, grinning from ear to ear.

"Congratulations. You better invite me to the wedding!"

Pablo laughed. "No plans for that yet, but knowing *mi mamá*, that won't be long."

"When do you go?"

"My flight is in two hours," he said, glancing at his watch. "The taxi service will be here in about fifteen minutes. I am glad you got home in time, so I could say goodbye. And congratulations on the article. It is very well done. That is what you were doing on New Year's Day?"

"Yes, sorry to ignore you. It was important to get the story out about what happened in the warehouse and Panama as soon as possible. It had waited way too long."

"Now it is history, and we can all move on," said Pablo.

"Yes, finally," Jesse said. "Time for new beginnings. Speaking of that, you'll never guess who I met." He related the story of Little Jesse.

"I want to meet him someday," said Pablo, standing up. "I must go now. The taxi should be here any minute. Next time I visit it will be with Lilliana, and we will celebrate."

Jesse got up from the couch and they hugged, slapping one another on the back.

"You've been a good *amigo*, gringo brother," Pablo told him, heading for the door and pulling it open. He hesitated and then swung around to ask, "What about you and Clare?"

As Jesse opened his mouth to reply, Clare appeared in the doorway.

With Pablo's words still hanging in the air, her face reddened slightly, but she managed to say, "Hello, you two."

"Very nice to see you, Clare." Pablo gave her a peck on both cheeks. He winked at Jesse and said, "I leave you in lovely hands," and then he walked out the door.

Clare raised her eyebrows at Jesse. "I hope he's not leaving because of me."

"He's got a flight to catch," said Jesse, approaching Clare. "I'm so glad to see you. Sorry I've been out of touch the last couple of days."

"You were busy writing. I saw the article. It's remarkable. I'm so proud of you."

"Thanks, Clare, that means a lot coming from you." Jesse paused, searching for the perfect words. "A lot of stuff I had buried deep came up while I was writing the article. Painful stuff, but good things, too. You were right. I was stuck in the past, and I'm still struggling to face things, but I'm ready to move on. And there's someone who's going to help me do that. You'll never believe who I met yesterday."

"Who?" asked Clare, studying Jesse's face.

"I met Randy's son," Jesse said and smiled.

"His son! Oh, my gosh. Missy?"

Jesse explained the whole story, ending with how he planned to take Little Jesse to a baseball game the following week.

"I'm so happy for you, Jesse! To have a part of Randy here, now. What an absolutely priceless gift."

Jesse didn't speak for a moment, and then caressed Clare's face with his hands.

"I'd like it to be us."

A crease appeared on Clare's forehead, and she tilted her head slightly to one side.

"I'd like people to say they're happy for us."

The questions in Clare's eyes turned to surprise. "What are you saying?"

"Since getting together with you again, I realized that I may have left the Canal Zone, but the truth is, you're my home." His voice became deep. "I don't want to wait any longer for the two of us to spend our lives together."

Clare gasped slightly and her green eyes widened. "What are you saying?"

Jesse took both of her hands in his and lifted them to his lips, tenderly kissing one palm and then the other. He looked up to find Clare's eyes brimming with tears.

"Would you marry me if I asked you?"

"Are you asking me?"

"I want to kiss you goodnight every night and wake up to find you beside me every morning." He struggled for a moment. "Will you marry me? Make me the luckiest guy alive?"

Clare silently nodded.

"No hesitations about marrying a Zonian?"

"None at all."

"What about Panama for our honeymoon?" Jesse asked.

Clare smiled. "I can't think of anywhere more perfect."

EPILOGUE

Jesse's story is complete. Sam's, on the other hand, is just beginning...

The taxi couldn't get to the airport fast enough. Sam Elvia strummed on the leather seat beside him with his fingers, thinking about the last 24 hours.

He was pissed at Jesse for outing him in the *Times* article, but he got it. Jesse had a job to do, and his conscience to clear. If he was in his shoes, Sam would have done the same thing. Randy would never want him to retaliate, anyway.

But that didn't change the fact that Sam was screwed right now. If Gonzales got ahold of him, he could kiss everything goodbye. And that was something he couldn't do to his mama—leave her behind. Not that he was number one son material, but he checked in when he could and made sure she was comfortable financially.

When the taxi finally pulled up to the Los Angeles International Airport, Sam threw thirty bucks at the driver and got out, his duffel bag in tow. He didn't have many possessions in the first place—liked to live light—now he barely had anything. That was okay. He'd get stocked up once settled in Mexico. Get himself another gun, too. Not being armed bothered Sam. Made him more skittish than he thought it would. His peripheral vision stayed on high alert as he made his way through the line to the ticket counter.

"Where will you be traveling, sir?" said a perky redhead.

"La Paz, Mexico. Give me your next direct flight."

It wasn't until the plane's engines reversed on touchdown at La Paz International Airport that Sam started to breathe a little easier. His Mexican buddy Juan Torino was sending a driver to take Sam to his house until he could get settled in his own place. The plan was for Sam to help him run his chain of bars. It was a laidback town and one of the last places Gonzales would look for him. He'd be safe here hiding in plain sight, with Juan's people covering his back.

After Sam passed baggage claim, he came across a line of drivers holding up cardboard signs. He spotted a beefy Mexican with a sign that said Torino. Nerves tight, he headed to the driver, cautious that one of Gonzales's men had been smart enough to tail him.

Sam reached out and took hold of the man's outstretched hand.

"*Mucho gusto*," he said as they shook.

"Nice to meet you, *Señor* Macaw," said the man. "*Señor* Torino is waiting for you."

See what happens with Sam "Macaw" in *Discovered Memories*...

A NOTE FOR YOU

Dear Reading Gem,

Thanks for spending time with me, Jesse and Clare, Alexa and Macaw, Brett and Tatiana, and Jessica and Spencer! While each of the books in the Discovered Truth Series can be read as a standalone, it's fun to experience the progression and get to know the characters. The series progresses as minor characters introduced in each book become main characters in subsequent books. It's exciting to see what they'll do next!

The Discovered Truth series features complex, gutsy women and equally complicated, charismatic men who find themselves immersed in dangerous and intriguing modern-day challenges, such as human trafficking, drug smuggling, national security threats, and identity theft. When the heroine and hero meet, worlds collide and sparks fly, kindling unforgettable romance and intrigue.

If you like the series, please leave a review and comment. Your opinion matters and is incredibly powerful.

Thanks again and talk soon!

Review this book:

Amazon

GoodReads

BookBub

STAY ENLIGHTENED

Thanks for reading! Let's stay in touch. In appreciation of you, I post updates, insider information, and sneak peeks of upcoming books on my website at https://www.juliebawdendavis.com/fiction. You can also email me at Julie@JulieBawdenDavis.com, follow me on Facebook, and find me on Amazon.

Even better, you can join my VIP Reading Gems mailing list here. I also created a Facebook group especially for you! Join Julie's Reading Gems to get the inside scoop on what's going on with the Discovered Truth Series. Find out how characters are created, and what they might do next. I also ask for Reading Gem opinions on character names. And there are contests and giveaways!

Speaking of giveaways, download the prequel to the Discovered Truth Series, *Discovered Beginnings*, for FREE by clicking HERE.

Escape to Unforgettable Romance and Intrigue...

BOOKS IN THE DISCOVERED TRUTH SERIES ROMANTIC SUSPENSE

Discovered Beginnings:
(FREE at https://www.juliebawdendavis.com/fiction)
Discovered Secrets
Discovered Memories
Discovered Indiscretions
Discovered Liaisons
Discovered Betrayal
Discovered Denial
Discovered Distractions
Discovered Deception
Discovered Lies
Discovered Vengeance
Discovered Redemption
Discovered Obsession
Discovered Transgressions
Discovered Suspicion
Discovered Escape
Discovered Promises
Discovered Cover-up
Discovered Intentions

Box Sets

The Discovered Truth Series Box Set Books 1-4
The Discovered Truth Series Box Set Books 5-8
The Discovered Truth Series Box Set Books 9-12
The Discovered Truth Series Box Set Books 13-16